THE WHISTLE,
THE GRAVE,
AND THE GHOST

John Bellairs's Lewis Barnavelt *in*

THE WHISTLE,
THE GRAVE,
AND THE GHOST

BY
BRAD STRICKLAND

Dial Books for Young Readers
New York

Published by Dial Books for Young Readers

A division of Penguin Young Readers Group

345 Hudson Street

New York, New York 10014

Designed by Jasmin Rubero

Text set in Janson Text

Printed in the U.S.A. on acid-free paper

3 5 7 9 10 8 6 4 2

Library of Congress Cataloging-in-Publication Data

Bellairs, John.

Lewis Barnavelt in The whistle,

the grave, and the ghost / by Brad Strickland.

p.   cm.

Summary: In the woods near his home in Michigan,
thirteen-year-old Lewis Barnavelt stumbles upon
an ancient grave and silver whistle that draw him,
his best friend Rose Rita Pottinger, his uncle Jonathan,
and their friend Mrs. Zimmermann into
a battle with an ancient evil.

ISBN 0-8037-2622-8

[1. Supernatural—Fiction. 2. Magic—Fiction.]

I. Title: Whistle, the grave, and the ghost.

II. Strickland, Brad. III. Title.

PZ7.B413 Lg 2003   [Fic]—dc21

2002010817

*This one is for the fans I've met
at compleatbellairs. Keep the faith, all!*

CHAPTER ONE

On an overcast summer afternoon in the 1950s, a dozen boys and one man, all wearing Boy Scout uniforms, hiked through a meadow in southern Michigan. The man had a grim expression, probably because all twelve boys were bellowing out a song:

> "We are the true Scouts, true blue are we,
> We are the Scouts of Troop One-thirty-three!
> We are the best of all of the rest,
> And as we march, we all sing mer-ri-lee:
> We are the true Scouts . . ."

Like "99 Bottles of Beer on the Wall," it was a song calculated to drive adults crazy in about thirty seconds. At the end of the line of boys, struggling to keep up and huffing and puffing rather than singing, Lewis Barnavelt clumped along. He was about thirteen, overweight, and nearly as unathletic as a boy could be. At that particular moment, he was exhausted and hot. Sweat trickled in tickling beads down his neck and stained his khaki uniform. The straps of his knapsack dug uncomfortably into his shoulders. The dry summer grass swished and crackled as he trudged through it.

At least, he thought, this was better than the woods, where the other boys liked to push branches aside and then let go of them so they'd spring back and slap him in the face. They laughed at him when the twigs stung his eyes and made tears roll down his cheeks.

Still, trudging through the meadow under the weight of his bedroll, tent, and supplies was hard, hot work. Lewis knew better than to complain, though. Others could gripe all they wanted, but one word from Lewis would mark him as a crybaby, and he'd never hear the end of it.

After what seemed like hours, Scoutmaster Halvers blew a shrill, rattling blast on his whistle. Lewis halted and looked up. The troop had reached the crest of a low, rounded hill. "We'll set up camp here," the scoutmaster said. "It will be a good location if we get rain tonight. First pitch the tents, and then I want some volunteers to fetch some rocks and some firewood. Peters, Fox, and . . . let's see, Barnavelt, you'll do."

"Fox an' me'll get the wood," said Stan Peters promptly. He was a tall, lanky red-haired kid with big ears, a big nose, and about a thousand pale orange freckles on his cheeks. "Let Barnavelt get the rocks."

"Yeah," agreed Billy Fox. Billy was shorter than Stan, and chunkier. He had a round face, brownish-blond hair cropped into a flattop haircut, and the solid build of a football player. In a voice soft enough for only Lewis and Stan to hear, he added, "Lard Guts needs the exercise!"

Lewis felt his face flaming. He shot Billy a murderous glance, but he clamped his mouth shut. Lewis had learned long ago that if he argued with these guys, they'd just be rougher on him later on. So he turned away from them, unshouldered his knapsack, and turned his attention to pitching his pup tent.

At least that was something he could do well. Lewis and his uncle Jonathan had practiced this part over and over in the backyard of the Barnavelt house at 100 High Street in New Zebedee, Michigan. Lewis had lived there with his uncle for several years, since his mother and father had died in a terrible auto crash. Now Uncle Jonathan was his legal guardian, and for the most part, Lewis enjoyed their life together.

For one thing, Jonathan Barnavelt was a magician. And he was not just a conjuror who hid handkerchiefs up his sleeves and pretended to make coins vanish, but a real sorcerer. He could create wonderful, lifelike illusions, complete with sounds and smells. Their next-door neighbor Mrs. Florence Zimmermann was a friendly, wrinkly-faced good witch whose magic was even stronger than Jonathan's. Life was never dull with them around.

Even so, at times Lewis thought he could use a little boredom. He was by nature a timid boy, though in the past he had found himself having to face strange and magical threats. In an odd way, he could deal with them better than he could with the everyday problems of life, like bullies and demanding teachers—and weekend hikes.

Lewis hammered the last stake into place and stood back. His tent was a work of art, taut and tight, its angles sharp and crisp. "Mr. Halvers," he said, "I'm finished."

Mr. Halvers was a tall, athletic man with a bulbous nose, close-clipped gray hair that was almost white, and black-rimmed glasses. He came over and inspected Lewis's work. "Good job," he said, clapping Lewis on the shoulder. "And you've showed these slowpokes how to do it! Okay, Barnavelt, we need some good flat rocks to make a fire pit. You know what to look for."

"Yeah," said Stan with a sneer. His own tent was sagging in the middle, like a carpet thrown over a clothesline. "And thanks just so much for showin' us *slowpokes* how to do it!"

Lewis didn't say anything. He just walked down to the bottom of the hill and into the woods. Now he was in for it. Somehow Stan and Billy would get back at him, as if by doing his best, he had shown them up on purpose. When he was out of sight of the other Scouts, instead of searching for stones, Lewis sat down on a fallen log with his elbows on his knees and his chin in his hands. For a few minutes he rested and fretted about his life, which was unusually hard lately.

One problem was that the Catholic church that he and

his uncle attended had another new priest, the third one in a year. The new one was Father Foley. He had come all the way from Ireland, and he was an elderly, scowling man who seemed to think that all boys were evil. Lewis was beginning to dread going to confession. The other priests he had known had all been friendly and kind, and he had liked them a lot. When they handed out penance, it wasn't too hard: a dozen Hail Marys, maybe, but not much more than that. Father Foley scolded him harshly for every little thing, and his penances were more on the scale of mowing the church lawn, cleaning out the basement, and washing the windows of the parish house.

Stan Peters went to the same church, but somehow he never seemed to get into as much trouble. Two or three times Stan had happened by while Lewis was working outside the church, and he had sneered and gloated and made fun of Lewis. Sometimes Lewis felt as if Father Foley were joining in with the boys who liked to bully him. Even when Lewis did a good job, the priest frowned at him as if he were Public Enemy Number One instead of a junior high school kid who really didn't mean to cause anybody harm.

Lewis's uncle Jonathan told him that you had to learn to deal with all kinds of people, and he wouldn't let Lewis out of going to confession. Lewis didn't know how much longer he could take it. He used to enjoy Mass, with its comforting ancient Latin ritual and the sweet smell of *Ad Altare Dei* incense. By the end of the service, he always felt close to his father and mother. Before leaving the church, he would light candles and say prayers for them.

But now he felt that all the saints in heaven were lined up behind Father Foley, all of them staring at him with disapproval the same way the priest did.

Lewis heaved a sigh. He'd better start looking for rocks, and he'd better do it before Stan and Billy came looking for him. He poked around and dug up half a dozen flat stones that would do, piling them up at the edge of the woods. Then he went a little farther into the gloom, searching for more. He didn't blaze a trail, but he kept nervously checking landmarks so he wouldn't get lost.

That was sort of silly, he knew. The Scout troop was only a dozen or so miles from New Zebedee. The little patch of woods and meadows was surrounded by farmland, and even if he got separated from the troop, all Lewis had to do was keep walking, and before long he'd come out in sight of a farmhouse or a road. Still, he felt nervous about getting too far away from Mr. Halvers and the others.

Still thinking of his troubles, Lewis pushed through some brush and found himself standing at the edge of a rocky clearing. In the center was a stone far too big for his purposes. In fact, it was nearly ten feet long and perhaps five feet wide, a long, flat boulder nearly oval in outline. Scattered around it were thousands of smaller stones, from palm-sized to pumpkin-sized. Maybe back at the end of the Ice Age a glacier had dropped them all here— but to Lewis it looked as if the rocks had been left by people.

But rocks were rocks. He hefted a medium-sized one and carried it back to his pile. A few more like this, and he'd have as many as he needed. Lewis pushed back through the brush for another stone, and another. Then, on his fifth or sixth trip, Lewis sat on the large stone to catch his breath. Only then did he notice that it had something carved on its moss-covered surface. The engraving seemed ancient and weathered, and parts of some of the letters were missing, as if eroded. But Lewis puzzled out a strange inscription:

HIC IACET LAMIA

It was Latin. Lewis had been an altar boy and had also studied Latin in school for more than a year, and he could easily translate the first two words: "Here lies—"

With a yelp of alarm, Lewis jumped off the rock. It covered a grave! Someone named "Lamia" must have been buried beneath it. Lewis didn't think of himself as superstitious, but he never messed with graves. At least not since an awful thing that had happened not long after he had come to live with his uncle, when he had tried out a magic spell and the spirit of a woman named Selenna Izard had been summoned from its tomb!

Hastily, Lewis stooped to grab one last rock. That would have to do—

He paused. Something glinted in the black dirt where the rock had lain, something silvery. Lewis dropped the rock and scraped the dry earth away. He revealed a tube of silver about three inches long and as thick as a fountain pen. Lewis picked it up, turning it this way and that. It was a whistle, packed with soil but untarnished.

Just then he heard a crashing in the woods. Probably Billy and Stan, he thought wildly, and he thrust his find into his pocket. They'd only take it away from him, and maybe beat him up if they thought they could get away with it. Lewis snatched his rock up again, staggering a little under its weight. He heard Billy and Stan off to the left somewhere. Ignoring them, he hauled his rock to the campsite, and Mr. Halvers sent a couple of other boys who had finished pitching their tents to help him carry the rest.

By sunset they had lit a campfire and had cooked hot dogs and a pot of baked beans. The threat of rain had passed. Overhead, the sky slowly cleared as the clouds drifted away, leaving a vivid pink patch in the west where the sun had gone down. Lewis finished two hot dogs and felt tired but full. As dusk came on, the Scouts began to tell campfire stories. Lewis heard the one about the escaped lunatic killer with a hook for a hand, and the one about the woman whose husband told her she could look into every room in the house except one, and more.

Lewis didn't tell any. He didn't much like these stories. They reminded him of things that had really happened, things that he could not even mention unless he wanted Mr. Halvers and the others to think he had a few screws loose. The stories didn't really scare him. Well, not very much, anyway. Lewis noticed that as the tales went on, the other Scouts huddled closer and closer to the fire, until he realized he was sitting all alone.

Billy Fox was telling a story about a hermit named Crazy Jake who had lived "maybe in these very woods" a hundred years ago. "So this hunter gets lost, see?" he said, making his voice sound hollow and spooky. "An' he comes to this shack in the woods. And this guy opens the door when the hunter knocks, okay? An' he's about seven feet tall with wild hair and a tangled beard so ratty that it's got grass an' stuff growing in it . . ."

The other boys listened, but Lewis idly took the whistle he had found from his pocket. He picked up a twig and started cleaning the packed dirt from inside the silver tube. Who could have lost it there? How old was it? Maybe a Potawatomi hunter had dropped it centuries before Columbus came to the New World. Maybe a French explorer had worn it around his neck in the days when the United States did not even exist as a country. Lewis liked imagining all the possibilities.

Billy was coming to the end of his story: "An' the hunter had never slept on a bed that soft. So he wondered what the mattress was stuffed with. So he takes his hunting knife and cuts a tiny slit in th' cover. An' inside is human hair! He jumps up an' goes to run out of the room, but he opens the wrong door. It's a closet. An' inside are piles and piles of human heads, an' they've all been scalped! An' just then he felt somebody grab his hair!"

Stan had slipped around the edge of the campfire. He seized Barney Bajorski's red hair and tugged it, and

Barney, who was almost as timid as Lewis, shrieked in alarm.

Lewis grunted, glad that he had stayed put when all the other Scouts had closed in around the fire. Otherwise *he* would have been Stan's victim.

He had picked most of the dirt out of the whistle, but it was still gritty and dirty. He decided that when the camp-out was over, he would ask his friend Rose Rita Pottinger to help him research his find. She was almost a year older than he was, but Rose Rita and he were in the same class at school. She was a brainy girl who liked history, especially if it had anything to do with cannons or adventures or exploration. In the meantime, he would clean the whistle up and—

He started. The Scouts were already dousing the fire, and Donnie Malone was playing "Taps" on his bugle, hitting about one good note out of every six. It was time to turn in.

Each of the boys crawled into the sleeping bag in his own tent. Lewis lay on his back, with his head just outside the pup tent. He had his hands clasped behind his head, and he stared up into the dark night sky. He could name many of the constellations, and he could see that two planets were out: brilliant Jupiter and red Mars. A half-moon rode up there with them. Around him, crickets were chirping, and from far away came the mournful hoots of an owl. A breeze rustled the dry grass. Lewis closed his eyes and soon fell asleep.

He woke suddenly some time later. He had the suffocating feeling that he was buried! His chest heaved, but he could not breathe! Lewis struggled, only to find his arms pinned down. He couldn't even move! Something was pushing against his face—

With strength he did not even know he had, Lewis bucked and shoved. He managed to drag some air into his lungs and screeched out a terrified, high-pitched yell.

"What's wrong?" It was the voice of Mr. Halvers, sounding sleepy and angry.

Lewis felt someone tugging at him. Then, suddenly, he could breathe again. Cool air rushed into his lungs, and he found himself blinking up at Mr. Halvers, who held a flashlight.

"What's the meaning of this?" demanded Mr. Halvers sternly.

"I—I—" gasped Lewis.

"Here." Mr. Halvers unzipped the sleeping bag, freeing Lewis.

Lewis crept out, still panting for air. He finally realized what had happened. Somehow, he had gotten completely zipped up in his sleeping bag, head and all. He stood trembling and, in the light of Mr. Halvers's flashlight, he saw that his tent was ruined. It sagged and swayed, and three huge rips gashed the canvas.

Beyond the little yellow circle of light, the other boys were grinning at him. Lewis saw Billy nudge Stan, and they both snickered.

"Who did this?" asked Mr. Halvers, shining his light over the vandalized tent. "Lewis, do you know?"

Lewis shook his head. "I didn't see anybody."

"Could've been a bear," said Billy.

"Or maybe Crazy Jake," put in Stan, as if he were trying to be helpful. The others giggled and sniggered.

"This is not the way a Scout behaves," scolded Mr. Halvers. "Who did this to Lewis?"

The boys grew quiet as the flashlight beam traveled from face to face. Nobody admitted anything.

"All right," snapped Mr. Halvers. "Forget about earning any merit badges for this trip. All except Lewis. Now go to bed. Lewis, your tent's in bad shape, but I don't think it's going to rain, at any rate. Can you manage?"

Lewis nodded.

"No more tricks," growled Mr. Halvers, turning off his flashlight. "Turn in. Now!"

As he settled down, Lewis was sure he heard some smothered chuckles. He lay with bitter anger burning inside him. If he were tougher, he'd show them! He'd teach them not to pick on anybody just because he was heavy.

He lay in his sleeping bag with his heart slowly returning to its normal beat. With the flashlight out, the campsite was bathed in darkness. Only a thin column of gray smoke drifted up from the dead campfire, looking ghostly in the pale moonlight.

Lewis closed his eyes. Then they flew open again. Smoke? They had doused the campfire with water! He rose up on his elbows.

Did he really see smoke? It looked like a faint, writhing wisp, about as tall as a man, but it was so hard to see that Lewis thought his eyes might be tricking him. He rubbed them. Now he couldn't see anything at all. Nothing but darkness and the distant stars and moon.

Anyway, Lewis thought, the campfire wasn't even in that direction. It was farther to the left.

He closed his eyes again. Then he had an unsettling thought. The boys had been telling ghost stories. What if it had not been smoke at all, but a ghost?

Lewis rose and stared again. Nothing. He lay back down.

But this time he knew he would not be able to sleep.

CHAPTER TWO

The Scouts got back to New Zebedee on Sunday after-noon. "How'd it go?" asked Uncle Jonathan as Lewis staggered through the doorway under the burden of his knapsack.

"Not so great," admitted Lewis. He unrolled his pup tent. "Look."

Jonathan had red hair just turning gray, a red beard streaked with white, and a kindly manner. He came over and handled the ruined tent. "Looks like someone did this with a knife," he said slowly. "What happened?"

"Some of the guys clowning around," said Lewis. "They thought it was a big fat joke. I'm sorry, Uncle Jonathan. I'll pay for it out of my allowance."

"Don't be silly," his uncle told him. "I can afford to

replace a pup tent! But this is worse than a joke. It's mean, and it's destructive. Who did it?"

Lewis hung his head. "I don't know for sure. It happened while I was asleep. I didn't see anything."

Jonathan looked at Lewis. "Okay. But I'm going to have a word with Fred Halvers. This would be a pretty mean thing to do to a boy whose parents didn't have the money to buy a new one." He held up the pup tent by its edges and sighed. "Too far gone even to patch." Then his eyes twinkled. "Of course, we could ask Florence to use her magic and make it as good as new. But that would be cheating."

Lewis nodded. Although Florence Zimmermann could easily do something as simple as patching a tent with a wave of her wand, she almost never used magic for something trivial like that. She had explained to Lewis once that magic was for important things. "Anyway," she had finished, "that would take all the fun out of it. Why, if I used magic to whip up a German chocolate cake, it would taste just as gooey and sweet as my home-baked ones. But I wouldn't have the fun of glopping and slopping the batter, and your uncle Weird Beard wouldn't be able to lick the beaters!"

"Well," said Jonathan now, "we'll toss this one out and I'll buy you a replacement this week. Need any help unpacking your camping gear?"

"No, thanks," Lewis told him. "I can handle it. And then I'm gonna take a long hot shower. I'm all sweaty and grimy and gritty."

A few minutes later, Lewis stood under a stream of hot water. His shoulders and legs were aching from the hike, and it felt good to let the shower ease the kinks out of his muscles. He finally finished his shower, toweled off, and went back into his bedroom to dress.

Lewis liked living with his uncle. One reason was this house. When Jonathan's grandfather had died years and years ago, he had left most of his money to Jonathan. Jonathan had explained that once with a wink and a chuckle. "That's because my brother, Charlie, your dad, was a real go-getter, Lewis. Granddad knew he'd make a good living for himself. And the old man couldn't stand our sisters, who were bossy and nosy and who both disgraced the family by marrying Baptists instead of good, steady Catholics. But I was the old boy's favorite, because he and I were a lot alike: fat, lazy, and too easygoing to worry about making money!"

Lewis knew that Jonathan had invested his money, and that the investments brought in a steady income. Back during World War II, Jonathan had bought the mansion at 100 High Street, and he had never regretted his purchase. It was three stories tall, and all the bedrooms had fireplaces in different colors of marble. Lewis's fireplace was of black marble, with a fire screen. His bed was a big, solid four-poster, with battlements on the top that matched the ones on the frame of his tall mirror. From the window of his bedroom, Lewis could look out on the Hanchett house across the street, and beyond that to the water tower at the top of the hill. It was a great room, and Lewis felt a little smug when he thought that probably neither Billy Fox nor Stan Peters had ever slept in a bedroom as neat as his.

Lewis tugged on jeans and a red striped T-shirt, then slipped into his sneakers. He had dropped the whistle on his bedside table, next to his Westclox alarm clock. He snatched it up and stuck it into his pocket, then hurried downstairs. "Okay if I go over to Rose Rita's?" he asked his uncle.

Jonathan looked at his pocket watch. "I suppose so. Be back before six, though, because Florence is cooking for us tonight. Invite Rose Rita over if you want. There's always room for one more!"

"Okay." Lewis banged out the door, crossed the lawn, and opened the wrought-iron gate. Then he hurried down the hill and over to Rose Rita's house at 39 Mansion Street. Back when Michigan was on the verge of becoming a state, the people of New Zebedee had hoped that their town would be chosen as the new state capital. They planned to build a fine governor's mansion, and they even named the street after the proposed building. But then they lost out to Lansing, so the street name was a little misleading.

Rose Rita's house was not a mansion, but it was pleasant enough, like all the other houses on the tree-lined boulevard. As he walked up to the house, Lewis heard the crack of a bat and ball from around back. He went around to the backyard and saw Rose Rita tossing a baseball up and hitting it. "Hi," he said.

Rose Rita grinned at him. She was a tall, plain girl with long, stringy dark hair and big round black-rimmed glasses. "Hi yourself," she returned. "Hey, you're just in time. Want to play some flies an' grounders?"

They took turns pitching and whacking the baseball. Rose Rita was much better than Lewis at both, but at least she didn't tease him. "How was the hike?" she asked when they had gotten tired enough to pause and rest.

Lewis made a face. "Kind of bad." He told about the mean trick the others had played on him.

Rose Rita's cheeks flushed red. "What a rotten thing to do! Who was it?"

Lewis shrugged. "I don't know for sure."

Sternly, Rose Rita said, "I'd bet you pesos to peanuts that it was Billy and Stan, right?"

"Maybe," said Lewis slowly. He hated to get Rose Rita involved. She tended to take charge of things, and if she walked up to Billy and Stan and demanded they pay for Lewis's ruined tent, he would be in even worse trouble with them. And they would call him a sissy and say that he and Rose Rita were in love with each other. He suddenly remembered the whistle in his pocket. Maybe it would distract Rose Rita, he thought. He pulled it out. "Hey, I found this in the woods."

Rose Rita took it from him. "A British police whistle?"

"I don't think so," said Lewis. "I think it may be really old. It was under a rock."

Rose Rita turned the whistle in her fingers. "It's got engraving on it," she observed. "Curlicues and loops . . . and some words." She squinted through her glasses. "S . . . I . . . these are hard to make out."

"Let me see." Lewis squinted at the silver tube. No wonder he hadn't noticed the letters. They were very faint, and in such a swirly script that it was hard to tell if he was looking at a word or just a part of the engraved design. Slowly he read, "*Sibila et veniam.* At least I think that's what it is."

"Latin?" asked Rose Rita. "'*Something* and I come'?"

"'*Something* and I will come,'" corrected Lewis. "But I don't know that first word. It must be a verb, and it's imperative, but that's all I know."

"I've got my dictionary upstairs," said Rose Rita. "I'll run and get it."

She lugged the big, black-bound Latin-English dictionary to the front porch, and they leafed through it with no luck. "Must be a rare word," muttered Lewis. "Maybe if we check the big dictionary in the public library . . ."

"Well, we can't do that right now," said Rose Rita. She picked up the whistle and raised it to her lips.

Lewis grabbed her arm, stopping her. "Don't put that in your mouth! My gosh, I told you that I dug it up from under a rock. It was in wormy old dirt and might have all kinds of germs on it."

"Yuck." Rose Rita stuck out her tongue. "Thanks for stopping me." She handed the whistle back to Lewis. "I just wondered what it sounded like. Maybe you can wash it or soak it in alcohol or something."

Putting the whistle back into his jeans pocket, Lewis said, "Oh, I was supposed to ask if you wanted to come over for dinner tonight. Mrs. Zimmermann's cooking."

"Sure," said Rose Rita promptly. "I'll go tell my mom." She carried the dictionary back inside and in a few minutes was back, clapping a Detroit Tigers baseball cap onto her head. "Let's go!"

They walked to High Street, then up the hill. On the way, Rose Rita asked, "So who do you suppose lost the whistle in the first place?"

Lewis shook his head. "I don't know. I thought it might be pre-Columbian or—"

"Nah," put in Rose Rita. "It wouldn't be native to America. Not with a Latin inscription."

"But I hadn't *seen* the inscription then," explained Lewis, a little irritated. "Anyway, some people think the Romans and Carthaginians came across the Atlantic Ocean centuries before Columbus."

Rose Rita laughed. "In their quinqueremes and galleys? That's very far-fetched."

"I didn't say *I* believed it. It might be something a missionary dropped, though. There were French priests here at one time, converting the Potawatomi and the—"

"Priests don't usually carry whistles, though," interrupted Rose Rita. "None that I ever heard of."

"Some of them might," insisted Lewis stubbornly. "Anyway, I found this near a grave."

"A what?"

"You heard me," said Lewis smugly.

Rose Rita stared at Lewis, her eyes wide behind her spectacles. "Where was it?"

"In the middle of Richardson's Woods."

"That's nuts," declared Rose Rita. "There's no cemetery in the middle of Richardson's Woods. It's just a stretch of ground that was too rocky to plow up for farming, that's all."

Lewis closed his hand on the whistle in his pocket. "Well, it looked like a grave, and it had the person's name carved on the stone. 'Here lies Lamia,' it said. Maybe she was some pioneer's wife or something." Lewis had a good imagination, and he added, "They could have been the first settlers from back east to come to Michigan, and she got sick on the covered wagon and died. And her grieving husband buried her and put a big stone on the grave to keep the wild animals off, and he carved her name on the stone."

Rose Rita rolled her eyes. "And maybe it was an ad for Lamia Brand Super-Sudsy Washday Detergent."

Lewis grunted. "Okay, okay. But it looked like a grave! And—" He broke off suddenly. "And, come to think of it, the inscription on the stone was in Latin, just like the one on the whistle."

"Oh, so you think the whistle belongs to a dead person?" asked Rose Rita with a trace of sarcasm.

"I don't know," confessed Lewis. "But they must be connected. My gosh, an ancient stone inscription in Latin, and next to it a whistle with a Latin inscription of its own, way out in the middle of nowhere. That can't be coincidence."

Rose Rita did not look convinced. They pushed open his gate. Lewis's nostrils twitched. Mrs. Zimmermann was a fabulous cook, and the aroma of the dinner she had prepared drifted out and made him drool with anticipation. It smelled like a pork roast, and there was the wonderful yeasty scent of fresh-baked bread, and maybe the spicy-sweet fragrance of a hot apple pie.

Rose Rita sniffed too. "Yum!"

They hurried inside. Mrs. Zimmermann and Uncle Jonathan were just setting the table. "Hello, you two!" said Mrs. Zimmermann with a wide smile. As usual, she was wearing a purple dress, and her untidy gray hair was piled up in a loose bun on the top of her head. "Just in time. Wash your hands and hurry back."

They practically ran. The food was just as good as Lewis had anticipated. Mrs. Zimmermann beamed to see how they dug in, and she chuckled as Uncle Jonathan took a big bite of apple pie and murmured, "Mmmmmm! Superb, Pruny Face! This is even better than the cherry pie you baked last month, and that was the best cherry pie anyone ever made!"

"Thank you very much, Brush Mush!" said Mrs. Zimmermann. "But don't think that compliments are going to get you out of washing the dishes!"

Lewis had to grin at the way his uncle and Mrs. Zimmermann traded their insulting nicknames. It was an old habit with them, one that often made him smile.

Mrs. Zimmermann smiled as she watched Lewis finish off his first piece of pie. "Well, Lewis, your uncle tells me that Father Foley is coming down a little hard on you. Are you going to late Mass?"

Lewis looked at his uncle. Jonathan said, "Missing one Mass isn't exactly a mortal sin, Florence. And Father Foley knew all about the weekend hike. The church helps to sponsor Lewis's troop. I don't think he needs to worry about dragging himself in tonight."

Mrs. Zimmermann served Lewis a second slice of the delicious pie. "Back when I was teaching school, I'd run into people like Father Foley from time to time," she confided. "Lots of teachers who were short and snappy with their students. Almost every one of them had had a hard time of it somewhere along the line. They'd taught in tough schools where most of the kids were trouble-makers, or maybe even they had been through hard child-hoods themselves. Don't let him get you down, Lewis. I'm sure he means well, and you know sometimes priests don't understand young people as well as they should."

Uncle Jonathan chuckled and stroked his red beard. "Sometimes they don't understand us old fogeys either. Last week Father Foley said the parish house was in des-perate need of new gutters and he hoped some of his rich parishioners would step in and pay for them. And he cast a very beady eye at me, so I suppose I'm on the spot. Lewis, I'll tell you what: I'll donate the money for the gutters, and maybe that will make Father Foley ease up on you. What do you think?"

Lewis took a big sip of milk. Then, very seriously, he said, "I think . . . I think . . . well, I think I'd like to have another piece of pie."

Rose Rita snorted with laughter and milk spurted from

her nose. Mrs. Zimmermann jumped up with a napkin, but Rose Rita was fine, and her laughter was infectious. They all joined in. It was a happy moment.

Before long, Lewis was wondering whether he would ever be that happy again.

CHAPTER THREE

Days passed. Lewis had not forgotten about the whistle, but he had not used it either. It was now quite clean. Lewis had indeed soaked it in alcohol, for a whole day, and then he had scrubbed it over and over again under running water. Oddly enough, he saw no stain of tarnish, as you would expect of something that had been buried under a rock for who knows how long. The silver tube gleamed, as good as new.

Or at least Lewis supposed it was as *clean* as new. It certainly did not *look* new, but ancient, just like a museum artifact that had been painstakingly restored, but that still showed the wear and tear of ages. The engraved lines were faint, as though the touch of fingers over the centuries had gradually all but erased them. Even the puzzling inscriptions were no easier to read after Lewis's thorough cleaning. At times they hardly seemed to be there at all, and Lewis would have to turn the whistle this way and that to catch the light just in the right place to make the letters readable. More and more he wondered what connection tied this whistle to the stone in Richardson's Woods. Latin inscriptions, but with strange words that seemed to be in no dictionary, a similar strange feeling that he got when thinking of either—the two things belonged to each other. He just knew that somehow.

Lewis had found an old beaded chain, like the ones that soldiers wore their dog tags on, and had looped that through the round hoop at the end of the whistle, but he didn't hang the chain around his neck. There was something about the whistle that Lewis did not like. The black earth had been packed in it, worms had no doubt crawled in and out of it, and just the thought of putting it in his mouth turned his stomach. And then, too, what if it had belonged to the person who lay in the grave? The very idea spooked Lewis.

On the next Saturday afternoon, he and three or four other boys had to report to the church to sweep the aisles and polish the pews. It was part of his penance. Father Foley had him work on the Communion chalice and tray, as well as the censers, all of which had to be rubbed with polish and then carefully buffed with a soft cloth. It was boring work, but Lewis didn't complain. It was better than using a handful of rags, a bottle of Old English polish, and lots of elbow grease to shine up all the pews in the church. Somehow, making the gleam come out on the silver surfaces reminded Lewis of the whistle.

Father Foley sat across the room at his desk, doing paperwork and scowling down at it as if it were a sinful boy. For some time Lewis tried to get up the nerve to speak to him, and at last he succeeded. "Father," began Lewis in a small voice, "may I ask you something?"

The priest had a round face, but not a jolly one. Deep lines ran from his nostrils and dragged the corners of his mouth down in a permanent curve of disapproval. His dark eyes gleamed out from deep, dark sockets under heavy black eyebrows, though his wavy hair was snowy white. "What is it?" he muttered, sounding more absentminded than disapproving.

"Th-there's a Latin word I was wondering about," said Lewis. "I couldn't find it in my dictionary. I w-wondered if you might know it."

Father Foley put the paperwork he had been studying aside. "Very well. What's the word?"

"*Sibila*," answered Lewis.

Father Foley froze for a moment. He raised one hairy eyebrow. "That's a very strange word to ask me about!" His voice had become suddenly harsh.

"I'm sorry," said Lewis. "I've tried to look it up."

The priest shook his head and put a hand over his eyes for a moment. He growled, "*Sibila*. What a strange word." He took his hand from his eyes and drew a deep breath. "All right, Lewis. Let's work it out. What part of speech, do you think?"

"A verb," said Lewis promptly. "Imperative mood."

"Giving an order or command," agreed the priest. "As in, ah, *Spiritum nolite extinguere*. Translate!"

Lewis began to regret that he had brought up the whole matter. "Uh, 'Do not extinguish the spirit.'"

"'Quench not the spirit,'" corrected Father Foley. "And where is that from?"

"I—I don't know," confessed Lewis. "Um, the New Testament? Paul?" He knew that was a good guess, since Father Foley seemed very fond of the Epistles.

"First Thessalonians, you little heathen," shot back the priest, looking strangely angry. "I'll ask you again after Mass tomorrow, and I'll expect you to be quick with chapter and verse. Now, *sibilare*, as it happens, is a verb meaning, um, 'to hiss.' Though why anyone would command someone to hiss is beyond me. Back to work!"

Lewis returned thoughtfully to his polishing. "Hiss and I will come"? That didn't make much sense. He decided not to ask Father Foley about the name on the grave. With his luck, "Lamia" would turn out to be the name of some saint or martyr that he should know, and he'd be stuck with dusting the pews or mopping the rest rooms as punishment. Meanwhile, Father Foley kept glancing at Lewis in a suspicious way, as if he thought he were up to something. Lewis tried hard to look innocent.

The day dragged on, but at last Father Foley finally set him and the other penitent boys free in the early afternoon. Lewis climbed onto his bike and rode over to the public library, a big gray stone-fronted building not far from the Civil War memorial. He wasn't much surprised to see Rose Rita's bike outside the building. She was kind of a bookworm, and she read voraciously, even over summer vacation. Lewis liked to read too, but he tended to

focus on one subject at a time. He would read a whole se-
ries of detective stories or adventure tales for a month or
six weeks, like those by Arthur Conan Doyle and Ellery
Queen, H. Rider Haggard and Robert Louis Stevenson.
Then he would get interested in something else, and his
reading would be books of astronomy for a while, or
books about ancient history.

Lewis climbed the stone steps and pushed through the
front doors. Mrs. Geer looked up over her half-spectacles
and smiled. "Hi, Lewis," she said in a soft voice. "You're
kind of late. We close in an hour and a half!"

"I won't be long," said Lewis with a smile. "Where's
Rose Rita?"

"The Reference Room, I believe," the librarian said.

Lewis went back and then turned to the right. The
Reference Room was much smaller than the stacks, the
big rooms with row after row of bookshelves. Lewis
liked the quiet nook, though. It had high, arched windows that let in soft green light filtered through the trees
outside. No one was there at the moment, apart from Rose
Rita, who sat hunched over a huge tome. A big pile of
books lay on the table beside it, as if Rose Rita had already
been reading for a long time. Her toes were hooked behind the legs of her chair and her attention was so caught
up that she didn't seem to notice Lewis until he came and
flopped into the chair next to her. Then she jumped.

"I didn't hear you," she said, her expression serious.

"Sorry. Didn't mean to startle you," returned Lewis.
"What're you reading?"

Rose Rita turned back a few pages, then pushed the reference work over to Lewis. He glanced at the title: *Great Poems of the English-Speaking World.* Then he frowned. Rose Rita had the book open to the first page of a poem by John Keats. Its title was "Lamia." He read the first few lines:

Upon a time, before the faery broods
Drove Nymph and Satyr from the prosperous woods,
Before King Oberon's bright diadem,
Sceptre, and mantle, clasp'd with dewy gem,
Frighted away the Dryads and the Fauns . . .

"Pretty flowery. What's it about?" asked Lewis.

Rose Rita lowered her voice to a whisper: "A monster!"

Lewis gulped. He felt a stirring of dread, and hated himself for being so timid. Oh, he could take campfire stories now and then, but he knew very well they were just make-believe. It was one thing to sit beside the red embers of a dying fire at night and hear Billy Fox tell some goofy story about a mad hermit who never existed. It was completely different to hear Rose Rita talk about possibly real monsters in broad daylight. Taking a deep breath, Lewis said, "And Lamia . . . ?"

"Is the monster," said Rose Rita. "She's some kind of serpent that can turn into a woman, or vice versa. I haven't finished the poem. I've found other stuff too, including a nifty ghost story by M. R. James that has a whistle in it, although it's just fiction. But look here." She dug another thick volume from a stack on the table. "I've marked the place."

Lewis took the book. He read the title, *A Compendium of Myth and Legends of All Nations,* and opened the volume to the place marked by a slip of paper. He immediately found the entry on the right-hand page:

Lamia (lā'-mi-ä): a female vampire. In Greek mythology, Lamia was a queen of Libya, beloved by Zeus, but punished by Hera. Hera caused Lamia to fall into a trance and kill her own children by drinking their blood. Her grief drove Lamia insane. She was further cursed when Hera took away her eyelids, so that she could never close her eyes to shut out the horrors she saw. Her body changed, becoming half serpent, half woman. Driven by her envy of mothers whose children yet lived, Lamia delighted in luring them away and destroying them. She could still assume the form of a beautiful woman, but had also become a bloodthirsty fiend who killed children and young men. Her name was used by the Greeks and Romans to frighten children into good behaviour, and has become a synonym for a female witch or vampire.

A hard lump had formed in Lewis's throat. He swallowed it down with difficulty. "B-but that's just a myth. There aren't any real vampires. And even if there were, one wouldn't be buried a few miles outside of New Zebedee!"

"The word can also mean 'witch' in Latin," replied Rose Rita. She dropped her voice again. "And we *know* there are such things as witches. There's Mrs. Zimmermann, who's a good witch, but there are also bad witches. That's the kind Gert Biggers wanted to be, and she almost killed Mrs. Zimmermann and me just by trying to become one."

Lewis nodded. Rose Rita had told him all about Gert Biggers, who had lived up in the northern part of the state, and whose hatred for Mrs. Zimmermann had ended at last when the evil woman was herself transformed into a tree. "Is that all?"

"Not by a long shot," said Rose Rita. "I looked and looked and finally found *sibilare* in a huge old Latin dictionary."

"It means 'hiss,'" said Lewis. "I found that out."

Rose Rita gave him a mildly surprised look through her round spectacles. "Yes, it does. But it could also mean 'whistle.'"

Lewis felt sick. "'Whistle and I will come,'" he said. "That makes sense."

"But *what* will come?" asked Rose Rita. "I think you'd better let Mrs. Zimmermann take a look at that whatsis. She's an expert on magical talismans and amulets and things, and it should be right up her alley."

"Okay," agreed Lewis. With his overactive imagination, he could just picture something huge and scaly creeping from beneath that rock in the woods and slithering toward him, called by the piping of that whistle. "One thing I know for sure, I'm not gonna blow this." He reached into his pocket for the whistle. Then he turned a strained face to Rose Rita. "It's gone!"

"You lost it?" demanded Rose Rita. "When was the last time you saw it?"

"I dropped it in my pocket this morning," murmured Lewis. "I'm sure I did. It was on a chain, but I didn't want to wear it." He stood up and felt in all his jeans pockets. Nothing but a handkerchief, his front door key, and his thin wallet.

"Where have you been?"

Lewis shook his head. "Just around the house. And then I had to go to the church to help clean. Then I rode my bike here."

Rose Rita hopped up. "Let's go. We have to look for that thing. If it really is magic, it could cause all kinds of trouble."

They rushed out, with Lewis staring intently at the floor of the library, the front steps, and the pavement and grass around his bike. No luck. He led the way back to the church, with Rose Rita pedaling along behind him and to his left. The whistle could have fallen out of his pocket, reasoned Lewis, when he was on the bike. But if it had, it was no longer anywhere on the ground that he could see.

They reached the church, and Lewis went inside. Father Foley was just leaving his office. "What is it?" he asked in an exasperated kind of way as Lewis came hurrying toward him.

"I think I might have dropped something," said Lewis in a small voice. "May I look for it?"

"Be quick," snapped the priest, holding the door open. Lewis took a fast look at the floor and even thrust his hands down under the cushion of the chair he had been sitting in. Nothing. He thanked Father Foley, who gave him a curt nod of acknowledgment. As he was turning away, Father Foley suddenly said, "Lewis!"

"Yes, Father?" asked Lewis, stopping dead in his tracks.

The elderly priest stared hard at him. "Where did you come up with that Latin verb?"

Lewis shrugged. "I read it somewhere."

"In a book?" demanded Father Foley.

"Probably," said Lewis, unwilling to discuss the whistle.

"Very well," said Father Foley, turning away.

Lewis hurried to join Rose Rita outside. "It wasn't there."

They rode their bikes back to Lewis's house on High Street, their eyes on the ground the whole way. Still no luck. In front of Lewis's house, they rested, leaning their bikes against the wrought-iron fence. "Well," said Rose Rita, "maybe it's for the best. Chances are it wasn't a mystical doohickey at all. It was probably just some dog whistle or something. Good riddance to it."

Lewis brightened a little. "Hey, that's probably right," he said. "'Whistle and I will come'! It sort of makes sense if it's a dog whistle, doesn't it?"

"Sure," agreed Rose Rita. "Maybe Lamia was even the name of somebody's faithful dog. In the old days of the pioneers, someone could've been heading west in a covered wagon and camped near New Zebedee. And in the dead of night, a huge grizzly bear attacked! The dog charged! The bear hit her with a swipe of its paw! But the settler had enough time to grab his musket and shoot the bear. Only the poor dog died of her wounds—" Rose Rita broke off. "What are you looking at me like that for?"

Lewis shook his head. "You made fun of me when I thought a settler's wife might have been buried under that stone. Now you've put a dead dog there! What an imagination. You can make a story out of—out of two beans and a rusty nail!"

Rose Rita sniffed. "I'll be a famous writer one of these days. See if I'm not."

"So, do you think we should bother Mrs. Zimmermann?" asked Lewis.

Rose Rita thought for a moment. "Well, it couldn't hurt, could it? She won't make fun of us, and if there was something spooky about that tin whistle, she'd be the one to know."

They went next door to Mrs. Zimmermann's cozy house. She welcomed them in with a smile. Lewis liked his next-door neighbor's living room. Everything was purple, Mrs. Zimmermann's favorite color: The carpet and the sofa and the chairs were all purple, and the walls were covered in pale pearly-white wallpaper with a pattern of purple violets. Even the paintings that hung on the walls had splashes of purple in them.

"Now then," said Mrs. Zimmermann after she had served them some lemonade and some wonderfully light meringue cookies that simply dissolved on their tongues, "you two either have something on your minds or up your sleeves, so I will ask politely. What's troubling you?"

Rose Rita looked at Lewis, and he began to explain about finding the whistle. He carefully described it, adding the translation they had discovered for the inscription and the bit about the flat stone in the woods with the words "Here lies Lamia" carved on it in Latin. Rose Rita chipped in with what she had been able to learn.

Mrs. Zimmermann thoughtfully touched a finger to her chin. "Hmm. Well, none of that strikes a chord with me. You don't usually hear of magical whistles, you know. Bells, yes, and spirit trumpets and such. In my study of magical amulets, however, I never ran across mention of an enchanted whistle. And of course I know about Keats's poem, but that's based on an old legend. Where exactly is the stone, Lewis?"

"It's northwest of town," replied Lewis. "There's a bridge, with a place next to it that was wide enough for Mr. Halvers to park the bus. Then we hiked for a couple of hours across some meadows to the campsite. The woods are downhill from that, toward the river."

"Yes, Richardson's Woods. I know just the place you're describing, but I've never heard anything sinister about it. I wonder if your uncle would be willing to let us pile into his antique car and go out to have a look at it tomorrow. It's probably nothing, but it sounds worth the trip. And you're right, Rose Rita. It could be a relic from pioneer days, or even earlier, when French explorers were passing this way through unexplored territory."

They all trooped next door, and Uncle Jonathan readily agreed to the trip. "We'll take off after Mass and make a picnic of it," he announced. "Rose Rita, we'll swing by your house and pick you up about twelve-thirty. Is that okay?"

Rose Rita, whose parents were Baptist, nodded. "Sure. We'll be home from church by then. Pastor Williams isn't very long-winded. Just give me a few minutes to change, that's all."

So it was all arranged. Lewis went to bed that night feeling relieved. Maybe, he thought, it was just as well he had lost the whistle. It was one less thing to worry about.

But in his dreams he saw the stone, with moonlight shining on it. He seemed to be standing nearby, staring as if fascinated. The stone began to quiver, and strange noises came from it, low moans and a kind of hissing. Faint red light shone from cracks in its surface. And something flowed from beneath it, something dark and rippling.

At first Lewis thought that somehow water was running from under the stone, as if a spring were beneath it. But the patch of darkness was not water. It moved beneath the moonlight, catching glimmers on its oily black surface. It crept over the rocks in the clearing, and Lewis stepped slowly away from it, as if it were a living creature and he did not want to attract its attention.

Then his feet rustled in something. Somehow the edge of the clearing was deep in dry leaves, though autumn was months away. The moving patch of darkness stopped. Then, incredibly quickly, it flowed toward Lewis. He moved faster than he thought he could. He bolted forward. He leaped up onto the mossy stone covering the grave.

The dark, shapeless form flowed into the dry leaves. They heaved and rustled. Then—then, somehow—they stood up!

Lewis felt his heart hammering. The leaves were cling-ing together, making a shape that was roughly human. It shambled toward him, its head thrust forward and slowly swinging from side to side. Moonlight fell on it, and Lewis saw that instead of eyes, the weird face of the thing had just two hollow pits.

It was blind.

But then it dropped to all fours. It lowered its face to the ground. And it shuffled closer, hissing.

It could smell him.

Lewis backed away, trying to be quiet. He came to the edge of the stone. He took a step down—

And felt dry hands close over his ankle!

With a gasp, Lewis sat up in bed. His heart thudded as if it were about to burst. His right ankle was all tangled up in the sheet.

He told himself to get a grip. With an effort, he straightened out the covers and lay back down, hoping that his hammering heart would slow down.

CHAPTER FOUR

Lewis shivered, though the Sunday afternoon was bright and warm. His uncle stood beside the mossy stone with the strange inscription and shook his head. "Never heard of this," he admitted, "and I've lived in these parts all my life. Haggy, what do you say?"

Mrs. Zimmermann looked very odd. Because of the hike, she had donned a pair of riding breeches. They were khaki, not purple, but she also wore a big floppy-brimmed purple hat and a purple sweater. She carried her rolled-up umbrella, sometimes leaning on it as if it were a cane. She walked all the way around the stone, her head tilted thoughtfully. "I've never heard of it either, but that doesn't prove anything. And I can't feel anything particularly bad or good about this spot."

Rose Rita gave Lewis a reassuring look. "Then there's nothing to worry about."

Uncle Jonathan grinned broadly. "I agree with Rose Rita," he said. "If Witch Hazel here can't sense it, it simply isn't there. Lewis, I think you can safely write this one off as a false alarm."

Lewis gave him a wan smile. "I hope so. Just coming back here makes my stomach feel sort of queasy."

"That could be hunger," observed Mrs. Zimmermann. She rolled up her sweater sleeves. "All right, everyone, stand back. I'm going to cast a little spell here just to make sure."

The others backed out of the clearing. Jonathan stood between Rose Rita and Lewis, with a hand on the shoulder of each. Lewis fought to keep his breathing regular.

In the clearing, Mrs. Zimmermann waved her umbrella in the air and chanted something softly. Instead of a normal handle, the umbrella had a bronze griffin's talon clutching a small crystal ball. The crystal began to glow, a pulsating purple light. From it a billow of pale purple mist spread, growing to fill the entire clearing like a dome. In the midst of this Mrs. Zimmermann stood, with the umbrella held straight out before her. She turned slowly in a complete circle.

Lewis blinked. Shapes were becoming visible in the pale mist, shapes like shadows. A shadow-deer leaped from the ground, began to fall, and faded. A shadow-rabbit hopped across the stone, then was jerked into the air by a diving shadow-hawk. Lewis felt the hair at the back of his neck prickle. He suddenly understood what he was seeing: the deaths of creatures within the clearing! Everything that had died there had left some kind of imprint. Mrs. Zimmermann was calling them all up.

But no human shapes appeared. After ten minutes Mrs. Zimmermann lowered her umbrella. The mist thinned and suddenly was gone. Mrs. Zimmermann walked toward them, shrugging. "No monsters, Lewis. Just ordinary woodland creatures, rabbits and deer and lots and lots of birds and insects. As far as I can tell, nothing terrible died here."

Lewis released the breath he had been holding. "I feel better," he admitted.

Mrs. Zimmermann grinned. "I hope you feel well enough to eat some sandwiches and cake. Because now that that business is over, we can get down to our picnic!"

They did, but as if they had made a silent agreement, they walked away from the clearing, up to the top of the hill where the Scouts had camped. There they spread out their picnic, and ate and talked and laughed.

But Lewis kept glancing down at the woods. Somehow he had a sick feeling that whatever had begun had not yet truly ended.

Tuesday came. That evening was the Scout meeting. Troop 133 usually met in the lunchroom of New Zebedee High School. The high school was next to the junior high, with an alley between the two buildings. Lewis showed up at seven o'clock, and Mr. Halvers greeted him at the door. They were the first two to arrive. Before long, the others came in too. That evening they talked about the camping trip, and the reasons why no one in the troop except Lewis would receive a merit badge for it. Then they talked about some ways the troop might raise money for next year's Scout Jamboree. Finally, as they usually did, they wound up with some games. Lewis was painfully aware, though, that no one was having much fun. Least of all him.

When eight-thirty came and it was time to go, he was more relieved than anything else. He and Barney helped clean up the lunchroom, and then Mr. Halvers let them out and locked the door. Barney turned into the alley between the two school buildings, and Lewis started to walk toward Main Street. He had not gone far before he heard Barney yell, "Hey, Lewis! Come look at this!" from behind him.

Lewis paused. It wasn't really dark, but the sun was down. He looked back into the alley but could not see Barney. "What is it?" Lewis shouted.

No answer. After a few seconds Lewis called out, "Barney? What's up?"

Still there was no answer. Lewis felt uneasy. What was going on? Had Barney hurt himself somehow? He was a clumsy enough kid to do that. With a sigh, Lewis decided he had to go check it out.

He had walked through that alley thousands of times, but usually during the day. Lewis felt his chest tighten as he stepped into the shadows of the alley. Everything was very quiet. "Barney?" he yelled, his voice shaking a little. "What's the matter?"

At the far end of the alley, you could turn left and head

toward the high school gym, or right and head for the middle school ball field. When Lewis got to that point, someone tackled him. He flopped forward, throwing out his hands. The air huffed out of his lungs as he fell face-down onto the grassy edge of the pavement. He heard someone running away.

Then Stan Peters's voice yelled, "You better not say anything about this, Barney!"

Lewis gulped for air. "What—what's the idea?" he demanded.

Whoever had tackled him pulled him up to his feet, with his arms held in a tight grip behind him. "We don't like smart guys," said the voice of Billy Fox. He was so close that Lewis could smell his sour breath. "We're gonna teach you a little lesson."

It was so dark there in the corner of the building that Lewis could see Stan only as a vague, lanky shape. "Let me go!" said Lewis furiously.

Stan stepped close and punched Lewis in the stomach, hard enough to make Lewis grunt in shock and pain. "That's one," he said. "Wanna help us count, fat boy? Wanna see how high we can go before you start crying?"

Lewis struggled to break free of Billy's grasp. "Nuh-uh!" chided Billy, pulling Lewis's arms up painfully. "It's just gonna be worse on you if you don't take it like a man!"

Desperately, Lewis kicked backward. He felt his heel connect hard with Billy's shin. Billy howled in anger and surprise, and Lewis threw all his weight back against him. He felt Billy stumble. A moment later Billy fell to the ground, and Lewis, off balance, tumbled on top of him. Stan was dancing around waving his fists like a boxer.

"Get offa me!" bawled Billy. "I think you broke my ribs!"

Lewis rolled away from Stan. He tried to scramble to his feet, and felt something cold under his hand. Without thinking, he grabbed it and lunged up to a stumbling run. He pounded down the alley toward the street, hearing Stan's feet slapping on the pavement behind him. Lewis burst out of the alley just as the streetlight overhead flickered on. He felt Stan swipe his hand down the back of Lewis's shirt.

Lewis twisted away and saw what he had picked up. It was the whistle, the chain dangling from it. He turned on Stan and yelled, "You better stop!"

Behind Stan, Billy came limping out of the alley. "Pound the tub of guts!" Billy yelled. "Hold him an' *I'll* pound him!"

Lewis knew there was no way he could outrun the two. He did the only thing that he could think of. He thrust the whistle between his lips and blew as hard as he could.

The whistle shrieked, a loud, piercing note. The sound of it was somehow icy cold, making Lewis wince even as he blew with all his might. The evening sky seemed to flash, as if a silent bolt of lightning had burst out right above his head. He saw Stan and Billy for just an instant, as though they had been frozen in a high-speed photograph.

Both of them had stopped dead in their tracks. Both of them had their eyes and mouths open wide in an expression of horrified surprise. For what seemed like a long, long time they stood like that.

Then Stan yelled, "Run!"

He and Billy did run, in opposite directions. Lewis was shaking all over. He took the whistle from his lips, but even though he was not blowing it, he seemed to hear a long, lingering echo of the terrible sound. He turned too, and ran in a third direction. He did not stop until he rushed through the door of his house.

Uncle Jonathan and Mrs. Zimmermann were sitting in the study, engrossed in a game of chess. Lewis waved at them and then hurried up to his room. He opened the drawer of his night table and threw the whistle inside. Then he sat on the edge of his bed, trying to make himself breathe normally. He wondered what had just happened.

Slowly, his jittery feeling began to settle down. Lewis told himself that Stan and Billy ran away because they didn't know where Mr. Halvers was. They might have thought the whistle would summon the scoutmaster, or even a policeman.

"They're chickens," Lewis told himself. "Bullies are all chickens."

Still—just the memory of that weird high-pitched sound, the wail of the silver whistle in the dusk, made Lewis's teeth chatter. Did the sound affect Billy and Stan the same way it did him? Was it simple fear that had chased them away?

For the rest of that evening, Lewis felt jumpy. But as time went on, nothing happened. Lewis took a hot bath.

He lay in bed and read. Gradually he grew sleepy, and when at last he put his book aside and turned off his lamp, he went to sleep at once.

The bad dreams he had expected did not come.

Wednesday morning was clear and warm. Lewis ate breakfast, then called Rose Rita. She agreed to meet him in the park at the west end of Main Street, and they both showed up at nine o'clock. The park was a round one, in the center of a traffic circle. The main feature of the park was a circle of white marble columns that enclosed a fountain that sent up a plume of water like a liquid willow tree. In another circle around this were marble benches, and Rose Rita and Lewis sat on one of these. In the sunshine, with busy traffic around the park and pedestrians cutting through it, Lewis felt a little braver than he might have anywhere else. He quickly told Rose Rita about the strange experience he had had.

She frowned. "Billy Fox and Stan Peters are a couple of jerks," she pronounced decisively. "They're nothing but juvenile delinquents. If I were you, I'd report them to the cops. What they did was—was assault and battery!"

Lewis shook his head impatiently. "Haven't you been listening? What chased them off was the whistle! I fell down and there it was, right under my hand!"

Rose Rita gave him a suspicious look. "Are you sure it was the same whistle?"

Lewis nodded. "I looked at it after I got back to my room. It has the inscription and everything."

"So how did it get between the schools? Could you have dropped it there?"

Lewis shook his head. "I didn't go there when I had it in my pocket. It's like it just vanished until I needed it, and then it materialized again."

"Oh, sure," said Rose Rita with a touch of sarcasm. "I don't suppose you could've dropped it in the church, and one of the other boys couldn't have found it, and then lost it again behind the schools? Doesn't that seem just a tad more logical to you than a super-duper disappearing act?"

"I don't know what seems logical," confessed Lewis. "All I know is that it was scary. Finding that thing, and then blowing it. I think that's what chased those two off, just the sound. It was like—like—I don't know. Like something that was alive and was angry."

"Okay," said Rose Rita. "Maybe the doohunkus really is magic. Did you bring it with you?"

"I don't want to carry it around," Lewis told her. "It's in the drawer of my night table."

Rose Rita got up. "Then let's go get it. It's high time that Mrs. Zimmermann took a look at it."

Lewis didn't argue. They walked to his house, and he went up to his bedroom. He opened the drawer. No whistle. Feeling a strange fluttering in his stomach, Lewis pulled the drawer all the way out of the night table and dumped its contents onto the bed. There was a St. Anthony's medal, a souvenir of his first Communion. He found a rosary that had belonged to his mother. There were five Indian-head pennies from the 1880's, and a deck

) 47 (

of cards with pictures of authors on them. There were two rubber bands and a small flat gadget he'd bought that was supposed to help him become a ventriloquist but didn't really work. He sorted through some smaller junk: little lenses from old binoculars, a stone arrowhead that he had found in a creek bed near the Waterworks, and a red pencil with a tiny picture of a ferryboat and the name of it, *City of Escanaba*, stamped on it in black. No whistle.

Lewis scooped everything back into the drawer and plodded slowly downstairs. He and Rose Rita went out into the backyard, where they sat in a couple of lawn chairs. "It's missing again," he said.

Rose Rita shook her head. "Something is screwy," she announced. "Are you sure you found the whistle last night?"

Lewis gave her an annoyed glance. "I'm not *crazy*," he said. "I didn't just imagine all that! My stomach still hurts from where Stan hit me. Look at my hands." He held them up, palms out. When he had fallen, he had scraped the heels of both hands, and the scratches, scabbed over now, showed plainly. "They would have beaten the daylights out of me if I hadn't found that whistle."

Rose Rita gave a theatrical sigh. "I don't know what to do. We could tell Mrs. Zimmermann and your uncle, but so far they've drawn a blank. What do you think?"

Chewing on his lower lip, Lewis thought that over. "Well, I hate to go running to Uncle Jonathan. I think he thinks I shouldn't be afraid of bullies like Billy and Stan. He's always telling me to stand up for myself more. I mean, if I could find the stupid whistle, that would be one thing. But without it, I don't see what Uncle Jonathan or Mrs. Zimmermann could do."

Reluctantly, Rose Rita nodded her agreement. "I suppose you're right. I don't like it, though. Look, let's snoop around and find out some more details about last night. Who was the kid who yelled for you?"

"Barney Bajorski," answered Lewis. "You know him."

"Red hair, lives across the tracks?"

"That's him."

Rose Rita sprang up. "Okay, we start with him. Maybe he's a witness. Come on!"

Lewis grabbed his bike. They stopped at Rose Rita's house so she could climb onto her own bike, and then they pedaled down Main Street, rattled across the railroad tracks, and found Barney's house, a tiny cottage with two little kids playing in the yard. One of them ran inside, and in a minute Barney came out, pale and frightened-looking.

As soon as he got close enough, he said, "Gosh, Lewis, I'm sorry! Stan an' Billy were gonna beat me up if I didn't call you."

"That's okay," Lewis assured him. "It wasn't too bad."

"Did you see what happened to Lewis?" asked Rose Rita.

Barney shook his head. "Not me. I got out of there as soon as Billy let go of me! I looked for Mr. Halvers out in front of the school, but he was already long gone."

Though Rose Rita asked some crafty questions, Billy couldn't tell them anything else. After a while they rode back to High Street. They climbed off their bikes in front of Lewis's house. Rose Rita said, "Well, we don't have much to go on. I guess we just have to keep an eye on things and—" She broke off and yipped in alarm.

Lewis looked quickly at her. She was staring up at his bedroom window, her eyes wide. He jerked his gaze there too.

He saw—or did he?—it was over in a flash—what looked like a pale, pale face, a face literally as white as snow, pressed close up against the windowpanes. It was there for an instant, and then it was gone.

But in that instant, Lewis saw with a surge of dread that it had no eyes, no eyes at all.

Just two blank, empty pits that nevertheless seemed to stare straight into his terrified soul.

CHAPTER FIVE

Lewis and Rose Rita went inside. They climbed the stair and crept down the hall to Lewis's bedroom door.

Lewis swallowed a lump in his throat. His heart thudded so hard that he was surprised Rose Rita couldn't hear it. He put his hand on the doorknob and felt it round and cold beneath his palm. Slowly he turned the knob. It gave a faint click.

He jerked the door open!

And released the breath he had been holding. Nothing was inside his room. Nothing but the ordinary things.

"Maybe it was a reflection or something," said Rose Rita, but her voice was a little shaky. "Or maybe we just sort of imagined it."

Lewis frowned. "My bed," he said. It was unmade, the

pillows tumbled, the coverlet and top sheet strewn across the floor.

Rose Rita peered past him. "What about it?"

"I didn't leave it in a mess," responded Lewis. "I always make it up. Somebody's been in here. Somebody broke into my room!" He did not add his other thought: Whoever it was must have been looking for the whistle.

But Rose Rita seemed to read his mind. "I think you should check and see if anything is missing."

Lewis spent half an hour looking over everything, from the closet to the mantel over the fireplace. Not a single item seemed to have been disturbed. The sheet and coverlet were the only things that were out of place.

Rose Rita tossed them back onto the bed. "Still no whistle."

Lewis shook his head. "No. And I don't think anyone went through the drawer where I left it. All the stuff I put back looks like it hasn't been touched."

"This is nutty," declared Rose Rita. "I never heard of a burglar that broke in and short-sheeted a bed! Or one that had it in for hospital corners and smooth sheets."

Lewis had no explanation either. "Help me and we'll make the bed up again," he said.

Together they made up the bed, then they went downstairs, just in time to meet Uncle Jonathan coming into the house with his arms full of paper bags loaded with groceries. Lewis and Rose Rita helped him put things away. Rose Rita, after she had stacked some cans of soup in the kitchen cabinet, suddenly asked, "Mr. Barnavelt, could you use magic to tell if somebody ever broke into your house?"

Jonathan raised his red eyebrows. "What a strange question! Do you mean, do I have some kind of magical mystical burglar alarm?"

"Do you?" asked Rose Rita.

With a comfortable chuckle, Jonathan said, "In a way, I suppose I do. For years and years, I never worried about burglars. Not in New Zebedee. But then there was the time that the late unlamented Ishmael Izard or his henchman snuck into the place, so I had second thoughts about protecting the house. As you know, I'm pretty good at casting illusion spells. Well, not long ago, I placed some on all the doors and all the windows of the house. If a burglar tried to creep in, he'd find himself waylaid by a wolf, or chased by a cobra, or bedeviled with bees. They wouldn't be real, but the burglar wouldn't know that!"

"Could you tell if someone had tripped one of the spells?" Rose Rita wanted to know.

Jonathan stroked his beard. "I certainly could, though not by checking a gauge or reading a dial, if that's what you mean. It's more like something I could feel. And just in case you're wondering, I *don't* feel anything of the sort. What's up, you two?"

Lewis coughed. "I thought some of the stuff in my room had been moved. But I might have been mistaken."

"Stuff in your room?" Jonathan stared hard at his nephew. "Anything dangerous? Anything valuable?"

Lewis felt his eyes widen in surprise. "Gosh, no! I

mean, I don't have anything dangerous up there. And nothing very valuable. Nothing a burglar would want, anyway. It was just that, well, my bed was messed up, like someone was looking under the mattress for something."

At that, Jonathan insisted that they all go up to Lewis's room. Just like Lewis and Rose Rita, he could find nothing out of the ordinary. "Well," he concluded, "maybe you just forgot to make up the bed for once. But let me know if something like this happens again. I'm pretty sure there's no evil magic going on. Florence is a wiz at detecting things like that, and if she says it isn't here, it isn't here. Still, there's magic and then there's deep magic. Just to be on the safe side, stay on the alert. Tell me if anything else strange happens."

"Deep magic?" Rose Rita's tone was curious. "What's that?"

Lewis thought his uncle looked a little uncomfortable as he hooked his thumbs into his vest pockets. Jonathan said, "Deep magic is old magic, Rose Rita. Ancient magic, from ages and ages ago. As a normal rule, any spell a magician casts doesn't last past that magician's death. Oh, there are some exceptions in the case of extremely powerful wizards, or in cases where the spell is magic shared by more than one sorcerer. But no matter how powerful it might seem, that's human magic. Deep magic is, well, *wild* magic, magic from outside."

"Outside?" asked Lewis.

Jonathan smiled ruefully. "Outside the world we know, I mean. Outside our universe, for that matter. It comes from some other dimension, or some other time, or some other space. Deep magic is not created or controlled by humans at all. There isn't much of it around, thank goodness. In fact, deep magic is so rare that I'm not even sure that Florence would recognize it right off the bat. Now and then some unlucky magician, usually one up to no good, tries to conjure some deep magic up and tame it, but it always ends with the deep magic winning and the poor magician being devoured by it."

Lewis must have looked stricken, because Jonathan immediately added, "Now, I'm not suggesting there's anything like that going on here! In fact, I suspect that the chances against it are better than the chances against my winning the Irish Sweepstakes. My advice is not to worry about it. Just keep a weather eye out for anything odd. As the Scouts say, be prepared, that's all."

Lewis nodded, but he was thinking that while it might not hurt, staying on the alert and trying to be prepared certainly wouldn't help him feel any less apprehensive.

In fact, he had the queasy feeling that it could only make him more jumpy, jittery, and miserable than ever.

However, for a few days nothing uncanny happened. Slowly Lewis began to believe that his uncle had been right, and that he had simply forgotten to make up the bed that morning. Sunday came, and he and his uncle went to Mass. Father Foley had a way of delivering Mass in a low, monotonous voice, and it was a warm day. The priest's droning delivery had a strange lilt to it, just a hint of a foreign accent, but it worked like a lullaby. Lewis fidgeted for a little while, and then he closed his eyes. Until his uncle nudged him sharply, Lewis did not realize that he had been dozing off, but when his eyes flew open, the first thing he saw was Father Foley glaring at him. Lewis sank down in the pew. He knew he was in for it.

Sure enough, at the end of the service, Father Foley made a beeline straight to Jonathan and Lewis. In a grim voice, he said, "Young man, I don't come over to preach in your bedroom. I don't think you should sleep in my church!"

"I—I'm sorry," said Lewis, his voice timid.

Father Foley grunted. "Mr. Barnavelt, I think Lewis's penance after his next confession might be a little lighter if he comes to the church this afternoon to help me out with a few little things," he said. "I leave it up to you, of course."

"And *I'll* leave it up to Lewis," Jonathan replied in a civil tone. "What do you think, Lewis?"

Lewis gave his uncle a weak smile. One of the good things about living with Uncle Jonathan, Lewis always thought, was that he treated Lewis more like a grown-up than like a kid. Now, knowing that he would probably only make it worse on himself if he said anything, Lewis only nodded.

Uncle Jonathan said, "Very well, Father Foley. He'll be here."

And so at two, Lewis reported back to the church. The priest sat him down at the desk in the study and placed a huge leather-bound book before him. "This is the *Confessions* of St. Augustine of Hippo, young man. A very important work by one of the fathers of the church. When you have read one hundred and fifty pages, you may go. I will ask you some questions about the text next week."

Lewis should have brightened up at that, because he loved to read. But St. Augustine's Latin was difficult to follow, and in the study, just as in the church, the air was warm, making Lewis feel drowsy again. The hours crawled by, and outside the windows the day grew dark as clouds began to build. At about five o'clock, Lewis began to hear rumbles of thunder. When he finally finished his reading, it was close to six, and the thunder was louder and closer.

Father Foley asked him a few quick questions about his reading. "Very well. You may expect a list of twenty-five written questions next week. I expect you to be able to answer at least twenty of them!" Then the priest dismissed him. Lewis pushed open the heavy church door and stepped out into a stormy afternoon. Rain was not yet falling, but boiling dark gray clouds looked as if they were about to burst open and spill out a flood. A bolt of lightning sizzled overhead, and instantly a boom of thunder made the ground shake. Lewis set off for home at a trot, hoping he would get there before the rain soaked him.

Halfway down Main Street, Lewis thought fleetingly of ducking into Heemsoth's Rexall Drug Store and calling Uncle Jonathan to drive into town to pick him up. But he was close to High Street, and then he just had to climb up the hill and he would be home. Lewis thought that the storm might not break at all. After that first startling blast, the thunder had not been quite as loud, and the wind wasn't really strong yet, just gusty. So he ducked his head and hurried on. The darkening sky made everything look weird and coppery. Lewis drove himself to walk faster, though he was beginning to gasp for breath.

He turned onto High Street, and with his head still lowered, he watched the toes of his sneakers as they bit away at the distance. Lewis made up a nonsensical little rhyme, just to take his mind off the thunder: "Pick up a foot and put it down, that's the way to walk around." He began to count his steps, again trying to distract himself from the threat of lightning and rain. At the foot of the hill, he looked up.

By then the wind was moaning in the trees, branches overhead were whipping furiously, and the first drops of rain were plopping hard onto the pavement. Lewis was just passing a yard belonging to a family that must have been away on vacation. Five or six newspapers lay scattered on the walk to the front porch. An untrimmed hedge surrounded the yard, and the driveway was on the far side of the hedge. Just as he reached the drive, Lewis saw movement from the corner of his eye.

Two boys stepped out, blocking his way. One was tall and lean, with a spray of orange freckles across his cheeks: Stan Peters. And the shorter, heavier one was, of course, Billy Fox.

"We been waitin' to catch ya outside," Billy said with a sneer. "Stan saw ya go into the church. We knew you'd come around this way. This time we got ya, Barnavelt. No cops're gonna hear you yell for help out here, not with the wind kickin' up like this."

Stan grinned, an unpleasant expression on his freckled face. "An' the garage at this place is nice an' private."

"You leave me alone!" yelled Lewis, feeling fear rising in his stomach. "I didn't do anything to you!" He looked anxiously up and down High Street, but with the storm about to break, everyone was inside. A sudden blast of wind ripped some green leaves from the oak and maple trees, and they whirled away through the sky like frightened birds.

Billy balled up his fists and took a step forward. "You're a troublemaker, Barnavelt. You're a fat tub of guts, an' you're a crybaby, an' we're gonna make you pay."

Lewis had backed away, but the two bullies were closing in on him. They weren't hurrying. Stan was pounding his right fist into his left hand. Billy was grinning and cracking his knuckles. They're enjoying this, thought Lewis bitterly. If only he had the whistle—

With a sudden inspiration, Lewis felt in his jeans pockets. Sure enough, his fingers closed on a smooth tube. He pulled it out and held it up. "I'll blow this again!"

Stan laughed. "Who's gonna hear it with all this wind? Go ahead, Fatty. Blow your brains out!"

Lewis did not hesitate. He put the whistle between his lips and blew as hard as he could. Again the cold, dark sound shrilled out. The world seemed to go black for just a second, and Lewis felt as if something had ripped the breath from his lungs. The sound stopped Stan and Billy in their tracks, at least for a moment. Then Billy made an animal-like growl of disgust. "Get him!"

Both of the bullies lunged forward, and Lewis jumped away. He was in the yard of the empty house, and he ran blindly up the walk and clambered onto the porch. But there he was cornered. He pounded on the door.

"Nobody's home, you dumb fat punk," taunted Billy. He and Stan were almost up to the porch. The wind had risen and the sound now was a shriek. Billy yelled to make himself heard over it: "They're off in Florida or someplace. Why do you think we picked this house?"

Something began to happen. The long, dark green grass in the yard began to whip around in tight circles, as if a whirlwind were springing up. The scream of the wind became a deep echo of the whistle, a piercing high-pitched note that went on and on. The rolled-up newspapers spun around and around. The weathered rubber bands holding them snapped, and they flopped open, lying flat just for an instant.

Then the swirling wind caught them, and they rose up in a spinning column. At first it was a flurry of white, but then it seemed to find a form. "Look!" Lewis yelped, pointing a shaking finger at what was taking shape. "It's coming for you!"

Billy looked over his shoulder and shouted in alarm. That made Stan spin around too.

The whirling newspapers were forming themselves into an eerie figure. It had a body, and arms of a sort, and a head, but no legs. Instead, the body tapered to a thrashing tail like a snake's. The whole thing gave out a dry, hissing, rustling sound. Lewis stared, transfixed, as the thing seemed to grow solid. He felt like screaming, but he was too paralyzed by fear to utter even a squeak. He knew the face—the horrible, eyeless face—with its blank expression and its wide mouth. He had seen it in nightmares, and he had glimpsed it in the window of his room. Now he saw it swinging back and forth on a long neck, as if questing for a victim.

Like a serpent, the creature slithered forward. It had a flickering quality, as if it were only half real, but it was solid enough to make a scraping sound on the walk. Some flying leaves hit it and did not go straight through, but lay plastered on its white surface. Both Stan and Billy backed away from it. "You can't run away," Lewis heard himself croak. "It's a ghost! It can get you no matter where you are!"

Billy screamed, taking strange, mincing steps backward until he hit the porch steps. He lost his footing and sat down hard, shouting, "No! No! No!"

Frantically, Stan yelled, "Shut up, shut up!"

The thing's terrible blind face swiveled, homing in on the sounds. As fast as a stroke of lightning, it swept forward until it was right in front of Stan. Lewis could not tear his gaze away. The thing reared back, towering over Stan by more than a foot. Lewis gasped. He felt rather than heard a kind of unearthly voice: *Mine!*

Then, as fast and deadly as a cobra, the shape struck. Lewis saw it hit Stan about chest high. Still shrieking at the top of his lungs, Billy jumped up from the porch step. He bounded past the monstrous thing and abandoned his friend, running madly for the street. The creature instantly turned and sped in pursuit, leaving Stan.

Stan dropped to his knees in the grass, clutching his chest and moaning. Lewis jumped off the porch and ran to him. "Are you okay?"

Stan turned a face pale with fear toward Lewis. He was blubbering and gibbering. The sounds he was making weren't even words, just gobbling, idiotic moans and mumbles. To Lewis they were like noises a maniac might make.

Lashes of cold rain whipped into them. The whole world dimmed in a torrent that hit the pavement so hard, it leaped up again in a knee-high spray. Stan staggered to his feet, his hands still clutched to his chest, and then he ran too, pounding away to the street and then down the hill. Lewis hurried to the street himself. Through curtains of rain, he saw Stan turn at the bottom, but Billy and the ghost—if that snakelike thing was really a ghost—were nowhere in sight.

Lewis opened his clenched hand. The whistle was no longer there, just a red streak where he had clutched the silver tube so tightly. He stood there for a moment, chilly rain pounding on his head and shoulders, soaking him. He hardly felt a thing. Thunder boomed again, making him jump.

And then Lewis began to laugh. It was a savage kind of laugh, almost like a snarl of triumph. Lewis had beaten them both! All alone, he had defeated two bullies, each of them stronger than himself. He had really taught them a lesson! Why, he had a power that neither of them could stand up against. That neither of them could even begin to understand! He felt as if he had suddenly grown taller and stronger. Thunder roared at him, and he raised his dripping head and roared back! Lewis shook both fists at the stormy sky. No one could ever pick on him again. Or if they did, he would make them sorry—

But then Lewis remembered his own horror at seeing the creature that the whistle had summoned. The stinging rain made him begin to shiver. He felt torn between fear and an evil sort of happiness that Billy and Stan were at last getting a taste of their own medicine.

And he felt something else, something that Father Foley was good at making him feel.

An overwhelming sense of guilt.

CHAPTER SIX

Lewis got home just as Jonathan was about to pull out of the driveway in his car, an antique black Muggins Simoon. Jonathan waved at him as Lewis ran up the hill and into the yard, and he backed the boxy auto up to the garage. A moment later, Jonathan came into the house through the kitchen. He was wearing a dripping yellow slicker, and he sent Lewis straight upstairs to towel off and change his sopping wet clothes.

Lewis did, shivering uncontrollably. In the bathroom he hurriedly peeled off his wet T-shirt and jeans. His teeth chattered as he grabbed a towel and began to dry himself. He tossed the wet towel onto the floor and grabbed another dry one from the shelf. He wrapped this around himself and hurried into his room to put on warm, dry underwear, jeans, and shirt.

When Lewis went back down again, he found Uncle Jonathan mopping up a puddle of water in the front hall. "Are you all right?" asked Jonathan with a worried glance.

Lewis nodded. "I think so. Uh, the, uh, rain caught me at the bottom of the hill."

Jonathan wrung out his mop into a galvanized steel pail. He looked almost angry. "I am going to have a word or three with Father Foley. It's one thing to be strict with really bad kids. It's another to keep you so late that you come home looking like a drowned rat just because you got a little sleepy during Mass!"

"Please don't talk to him," said Lewis. "It was kind of my own fault." He explained about having to read the book in the stuffy church study and about how long it had taken him. He said nothing about Stan and Billy. "So," he finished, "if I hadn't been so sleepy, I would've finished sooner and would've been home before the storm hit."

"All right," agreed Jonathan with evident reluctance, putting his mop on his shoulder as if he were a soldier and it were a rifle. "I don't want to make things worse for you than they already are. Do me a favor and dump out this water."

That night they had dinner alone. Jonathan was not a very good cook, and the meal he put together wasn't terribly tasty. They had chicken noodle soup and roast beef sandwiches, but the canned soup was very salty and the roast beef was dry and stringy. Dessert was half of a rhubarb pie that Mrs. Zimmermann had made earlier, and Jonathan had two big pieces. Lewis had just a little slice, because he wasn't particularly fond of the sweet-sour taste. The storm had blown over by the time they finished doing the dishes. Jonathan suggested playing some card games, but Lewis was too exhausted. He went to bed early, and before long he fell asleep.

If he had any dreams, he did not remember them. But at midnight, he awoke suddenly. He opened his eyes, and the first thing he saw was the glowing dial of his bedside alarm clock, the green hands pointing straight up. For a moment he lay in bed wondering what had happened. Then he heard a strangled cry! Then another, and another! Leaping up, Lewis ran out into the hall. The noises were coming from his uncle's room. Lewis banged on the door. "Uncle Jonathan! Are you okay?"

The shouting stopped abruptly, and a moment later, Jonathan opened the door. He was wearing baggy red pajamas, the ones that he said made him look like a ripe tomato, and his hair and beard were all mussed up, with spikes sticking every which way. He gave Lewis a weak, embarrassed smile. "Sorry! Just a nightmare, that's all. I had the silly notion that a great big ivory-colored snake was slithering around beside my bed. I think it must have been a king cobra! Anyway, I dreamed that I woke up and actually saw the creature right beside my pillow, all reared up and ready to sink its fangs into me. Then you knocked and I woke up for real!"

Lewis stared. Beads of sweat stood on his uncle's face. "A snake?" Lewis asked in a small voice.

Jonathan patted him on the shoulder. "I simply had a bad dream. I have them now and then, usually after I eat the wrong food before going to bed. I guess the rhubarb pie was a mistake!"

When he got back to his room, Lewis lay in bed wondering if his uncle's experience had really been just a dream. Was the snaky creature that had materialized from the newspapers still around? Could it have followed him home? Did it know where he lived? Lewis closed his eyes and imagined he heard a low, slithery hissing. He held his breath, but still couldn't tell whether the sound was all in his head or really came from somewhere in the room. With his breath coming in short gasps, he turned on his bedside lamp.

Nothing.

With a sigh, Lewis realized he probably was going to have a hard time getting back to sleep. From his bedside table he picked up a book he had started to read, *A Guide to the Planets* by Patrick Moore. Uncle Jonathan had been talking about trying to take some photos of the moon and planets with their backyard telescope, and the book was all about observing Mars, Venus, and the other heavenly bodies and taking pictures of them. Usually Lewis found it an interesting subject, but he could not keep his mind on the planets and stars at all. At least, though, reading the same paragraph over and over again made him feel drowsy. He finally fell asleep with the book open across his chest.

And in his dreams the slithery sounds became hissing words. Words that he could not understand, but that seemed to threaten his life.

That seemed to threaten his very soul.

*　*　*

"There's something bad going on," insisted Rose Rita the next day as the two of them sat on the porch of her house. "I know it and you know it. It may not be any kind of magic that Mrs. Zimmermann can make sense of, but it's bad. You've got to get rid of that stupid whistle, Lewis."

Lewis had told her about his latest encounter with Billy and Stan. He had left out a few things, though, like the creepy way the newspapers had formed themselves into a figure. He had made it seem as if the whistle had just called up a storm and had scared them away. Now, with his head achy and his eyes swollen from lack of sleep, he mumbled, "How can I? It's not here anymore. It shows up when it wants to, and then it goes away."

"When *it* wants to?" Rose Rita pushed her glasses up on her nose. Her expression was furious. "That's crazy! How can a whistle want to do something?"

Lewis just shook his head. It felt wobbly, as if his brain were sloshing around loose inside his skull. "I don't know."

Rose Rita jumped up from the porch swing. She waved her arms in the air. "The next time the dumb thing shows up, throw it away!"

Lewis closed his eyes. The headache pounded in his temples. How could he explain? The only times he had the whistle were times when he was facing a threat of some sort. Asking him to throw it away then was like asking a starving man to throw away a juicy hamburger! Like asking a drowning man to throw away a life preserver! It was something he could not do.

"Let's talk to Mrs. Zimmermann again," suggested

Rose Rita. "I'm really starting to worry about you. You look like something the cat dragged in, then dragged right back out again. Are you sick or something?"

Lewis opened his eyes. The day was sunny and fresh after the rain of the evening before. But the light almost hurt Lewis's eyes, and the air somehow didn't feel right. It was as if he felt a chill, even though the sun was warm and bright. "I don't feel sick exactly. I just feel . . ." Lewis groped for the words. "*Weird.* Like I'm only half here. I'm tired and everything seems to take so much effort. I don't know what it is."

"Could be flu," said Rose Rita confidently. "There was something on the radio this morning about some kind of summer flu. There's already a couple of cases in the hospital. Do you have a fever?"

"I don't think so," said Lewis. His heart had thumped strangely, and a thought, almost like someone else's soft voice speaking inside his head, had come to him: *This is revenge.* It was like the voice he had imagined when the ghost was attacking Stan.

Rose Rita sat beside him on the swing again and put her hand against his forehead. "You don't feel warm. Just the opposite. Kind of cold and clammy."

"Maybe I'm just tired." A disturbing thought suddenly came to Lewis. "What did you say about the radio?"

"Huh?" Rose Rita blinked. "Oh, the local news report this morning. It just said that there were a couple of people in the hospital with some kind of flu bug, that's all."

Revenge, came the imagined voice, fainter but sounding triumphant. Lewis felt dizzy. "Who?" he demanded.

Rose Rita frowned and shrugged. "I don't think it said."

Lewis got up. "Could I use your phone?"

"Sure," said Rose Rita. "Come on."

The Pottinger telephone was on a little table beside the stairway up to the second floor. Lewis got the New Zebedee phone book, a slim volume, and leafed through until he found the page with "Fox" on it. "What's Billy Fox's dad's name?" he asked.

"Phil, I think," replied Rose Rita. "He works over at—"

"Here it is," said Lewis. "It's 2-3432." He dialed the number and then listened as the phone rang twice, three times—

"Hello?" answered an old lady's voice.

"Uh, hello," said Lewis. "Uh, is Billy there, please?"

There was a pause. Then the woman said, "Billy is very sick. He's in the hospital, and his mother and father are there with him. This is his grandmother."

"Thank you," whispered Lewis, and he hung up the phone.

"What's the matter?" demanded Rose Rita. "You've gone as pale as a gho—pretty pale."

Lewis confided, "I think I know who the two flu patients are. I think it's Stan and Billy." Lewis's chest tightened. "Oh, my gosh. Rose Rita, I *can't* just get rid of the whistle. What if it's turned some magic creature loose? If there's a spell to get rid of the creature, the spell might have to have the whistle to work!"

"It could be a coincidence," said Rose Rita in an uncertain tone. "You said that it was raining hard. Maybe Billy got sick from being soaked—"

"You don't believe that."

"No," admitted Rose Rita. "I guess I don't."

They walked back out onto the porch. Lewis said, "I'm scared, Rose Rita. Uncle Jonathan had a terrible nightmare last night. What if this thing is starting to affect other people? Uncle Jonathan said something about deep magic, about how hard it is to control. If deep magic attacks magicians, then Uncle Jonathan and Mrs. Zimmermann could be victims."

"What are you going to do?" asked Rose Rita.

"I'm going to try to find out what's wrong with Billy," replied Lewis. "And I'm going to try to find out what can be done with the whistle the next time it shows up. When I know more, then maybe I'll know whether it's safe to involve Uncle Jonathan and Mrs. Zimmermann."

"I'll help," said Rose Rita promptly.

Lewis gave her a look of pure gratitude. But then he frowned. "It might be dangerous. I'm scared out of my wits!"

"I'm not happy about it myself. But I'd be a pretty poor kind of friend if I ditched you because of some heebie-jeebie ghost snake! Okay, let's make our plans."

Their plans, Lewis could not help thinking, were hardly brilliant. As Rose Rita quickly pointed out, the public library offered very little help. Lewis's uncle had a collection of books on magical subjects, but he didn't like Lewis to read them. Years before, trying to show off for a boy named Tarby Corrigan, Lewis had read a potent spell from one of the more dangerous books. As a result, a long-dead woman had come back from the grave and had very nearly taken the life of Lewis and Jonathan. Since that time, Jonathan had moved some of the collection to a locked bookcase.

Still, the study in the Barnavelt house held shelf after shelf of books that told *about* magic without telling you how to *do* magic. They would start there, Rose Rita decided. If they turned up nothing, maybe the Museum of Magic, run by their friend Mr. Robert Hardwick, might have something. Mr. Hardwick had an extensive library of books on magic, though almost all of them were just about conjuring tricks and sleight of hand. Lewis had his doubts about finding anything useful there, but it might be a last resort.

Jonathan Barnavelt and Mrs. Zimmermann always went to the weekly meetings of the Capharnaum County Magicians Society, and one was coming up. That would give them a chance to dig into some works about magic, ghosts, and spells that summoned magical beings or creatures.

Meanwhile, Lewis and Rose Rita climbed onto their bikes and pedaled over to the New Zebedee Hospital, a renovated old mansion not far from the library. Inside, they approached a woman wearing a crisp white nurse's uniform. Swirly red letters embroidered on the front of it identified her as Doris Engels. Lewis was feeling nervous, and he didn't like the smell of the hospital. It was like alcohol and iodine, and it reminded him of illness and suffering.

But at least Nurse Engels looked friendly. She was young, with dark hair tucked neatly up beneath her nurse's cap, and she wore round spectacles that looked a lot like Rose Rita's. The nurse was sitting at a desk marked "Information," and she was making notes in a huge book like a ledger. She glanced up at Lewis and Rose Rita and asked politely, "May I help you?"

"Hi," said Rose Rita. "We're here to see our friend Billy Fox. We heard he was sick."

"Fox," echoed Nurse Engels. She looked at her book, then shook her head. "Billy is here, but he can't have any visitors right now. You see, the doctors aren't sure what he has or how contagious it might be."

"Is he okay?" asked Lewis anxiously.

"He's stable," replied Nurse Engels. Then, as if responding more to Lewis's worried expression than to his question, she added, "I mean he's not getting any worse. He's just not getting better yet."

"How about Stan Peters?" asked Rose Rita. "I heard he was sick too. Is he here?"

Again the nurse consulted her ledger. "Yes, he is. His symptoms are about the same as Billy's. They're friends, so they probably caught some germ while they were together."

"They're going to be all right, aren't they?" asked Lewis.

Nurse Engels smiled reassuringly. "I'm positive they will be. They'll get the best of care here."

Rose Rita jerked her head in a way that meant "follow me." She led the way to the waiting room. There she sat on a banged-up maroon leather chair with splits in its upholstery mended with plastic tape. "I think we ought to find out what's wrong with them," she said.

"How?"

Rose Rita scratched her nose thoughtfully. "Well, if this was the movies, we'd find a closet with doctors' gowns and stuff in it, and we'd dress up like doctors and nobody would think twice about it."

"That's crazy," objected Lewis. "We might as well put on those furry caps with the tails and tell everyone we're Davy Crockett and Daniel Boone."

Rose Rita nodded. "You're right. This is real life, and people know there aren't any doctors as young as we are. Hmm." For a few moments Rose Rita was silent. Then she grinned. "But you know something? There are girls who help the nurses, and they aren't much older than we are! And I think Sally Merryweather's older sister Phyllis is one. Let's go. I'll bet you anything I can find out about this. Sally loves to talk! I'll just have to wait for the chance to get her started."

Lewis spent most of that afternoon worrying and trying to stay out of his uncle's way. Jonathan was involved in some kind of legal transaction. It had to do, he had explained, with reviewing the stocks and bonds and other investments that brought him his income. "I only have to do this once every other year or so," he had observed, "but it's a pain!"

So while Jonathan scribbled and clicked off numbers on a battered old adding machine as he consulted folders and brochures in his study, Lewis tried to watch TV or read. He could not concentrate on either. Late that afternoon, Rose Rita rode over on her bike, and the two of them went to the backyard. "Well?" Lewis asked.

Rose Rita rolled her eyes. "Sally is a real motormouth! But I was right about her sister. She's a volunteer at the hospital, and when she got home this afternoon, she told her family all about Billy and Stan. They're suffering from anemia."

Lewis frowned. "Anemia?"

"That's kind of like loss of blood," explained Rose Rita. "Their red corpuscles aren't corpuscling, or whatever you call it. So they're pretty weak. Both of them had to have a blood transfusion. The funny thing is, when those two got home yesterday, soaking wet, they didn't have any memory of what happened to them. They were confused and acted so strange that their parents were worried. And Billy was pale and shaky, so his folks took him straight to the emergency room, and the doctors stuck him right into the hospital. Billy's folks knew that he'd been hanging out with Stan, so they called Stan's mom, and by that time Stan was so sick that they brought him in too."

"Rose Rita," said Lewis miserably, "what did that book say about the lamia? That it was a female vampire? Was that it?"

Rose Rita's expression became serious. She folded her arms as if she were hugging herself, or trying to keep warm. "That was it."

They stared at each other. Lewis couldn't even bring himself to ask the question that had come into his mind.

What if Billy and Stan were not suffering from anemia at all?

What if some ghostly creature was drinking their blood?

CHAPTER SEVEN

Luckily, that week the meeting of the Capharnaum County Magicians Society was at the home of one of the other members, not Jonathan's or Mrs. Zimmermann's. Lewis, Uncle Jonathan, and Mrs. Zimmermann had an early dinner, and then the two adults left for their meeting. Lewis immediately telephoned Rose Rita, and she was at the house on High Street within ten minutes.

"Okay," said Lewis as they began to look through the books. "We'll see if we can dig up any information on lamias or lamiae or whatever you call them. Did Sally say anything about Billy and Stan today?"

"They're about the same," answered Rose Rita. She had pulled down a big black-bound volume.

Lewis recognized it at once, even before Rose Rita opened the cover. It was a bound copy of Mrs. Zimmermann's doctoral dissertation, the research paper she had written when she was studying magic in Germany. Mrs. Zimmermann had several, and she had given one to Jonathan. "That won't help," said Lewis. "You know Mrs. Zimmermann said she'd never heard of a magical whistle."

"Maybe she forgot," argued Rose Rita. "It's been a long time since she wrote this, you know."

The book was really a bound typescript. Rose Rita opened to the title page:

Amulets

by F. H. Zimmermann D. Mag. A.
A FREE INQUIRY INTO
THE PROPERTIES OF MAGIC AMULETS

A dissertation submitted to the Faculty of Magic Arts
of the University of Göttingen,
in partial fulfillment of the requirements
for the Degree of
DOCTOR MAGICORUM ARTIUM
(DOCTOR OF MAGIC ARTS)
by Florence Helene Zimmermann
June 13, 1922

English Language Copy.

"Okay," said Lewis. "Maybe you're right. She wrote that more than thirty years ago. But I'm going to look in the *Directory of Magical Creatures*."

For several minutes, the two read silently. Lewis sat in his uncle's chair, with the green-shaded lamp shining on the page in front of him. Rose Rita had settled in the big wing armchair, and she held the dissertation close to her nose as she leafed through it. Usually Lewis enjoyed the dusty, faintly spicy smell of old books, but tonight it seemed to overpower him, making him feel nauseous.

The book he was consulting had no entry under *lamia*. However, under *vampire* it had an enormously long article, detailing vampires from different countries and different cultures. There was the *nosferatu*, although the text said that was a mistranslation of a word that meant "unclean spirit." This kind of vampire was a sort of ghost on the borderline between life and death. It was a bloodthirsty phantom still animating a dead body.

Others were even stranger and more disturbing. In Malaysia, some people believed in a creature called the *penang-galen*. Although this kind of vampire looked human, it could detach its head from its body. The head, trailing the monster's stomach and intestines behind it, flew through the air and sought out victims to feed upon. An illustration almost turned Lewis's own stomach. He could just picture this slimy creature sailing through the night air . . . ugh!

He quickly turned the page. A vampiric spirit native to the Caribbean, he discovered, was the *lou-garou*, which could take the form of a "hot steam," a tall, pale blue flame burning in the middle of a path or road. An unlucky person who blundered into the flame would collapse, all the blood drained from his body. The *lou-garou* would then return to a tomb, where the body that held its spirit rested. Lewis looked up from the page. "This is hard. I think every country in the world has its own kind of vampire!" He looked back down at the page. "*Wurdalaks* and *strigoi* and *m'rani* and . . ."

Rose Rita's eyes were serious behind her round spectacles. "Well, my job's not any easier. Mrs. Zimmermann classifies amulets every way you can think of. Stone amulets and silver ones, large amulets and small, plain ones and fancy ones with the Ivy League design and the belt in the back! I think I'm going to read all about the silver ones first. Get back to your book."

Lewis nodded, but the more he read, the more the old house seemed to creak around him. Some of the descriptions made the flesh of his arms crinkle up. Sometimes he hastily turned a page when a particularly fearsome drawing appeared. Finally, though, he spotted the word *lamiae* and bent close to the desk to read it. "Listen to this," he said. "'The Greek *lamiae*, or vampiric witches, may be related to one of the very oldest legends of vampires, that of Lilith. In Hebrew tradition, Lilith was the first wife of Adam. Because she refused to obey Adam as his wife, she was cast out of the Garden of Eden and Eve was created. Lilith became a vengeful monster, capable of changing her form. Sometimes she took the shape of an owl in order to fly through the night. By reputation, she is a drinker of blood.'"

"Okay," said Rose Rita. "So how do you kill her?"

Lewis read on silently for a few minutes. "It doesn't tell. But get this: 'The Greek *lamia*, a vengeful, blood-drinking magical spirit, may be a development of the Lilith story. However, according to tradition, *lamiae* may occasionally be tamed, or rather enslaved. In the year 1587, the French mystic and priest Pere d'Anjou was supposed to have captured a *lamia* by means of a magic spell, and to have held it through a mystical item of some kind. D'Anjou used the spirit as a weapon, sending it forth against his enemies. In 1611, d'Anjou, whose physical appearance was still that of a young man despite his being well into his seventies, embarked on a voyage of discovery to the New World, where he was lost somewhere in North America.'"

Rose Rita wrinkled her nose. "So? Did he come to Michigan?"

"Doesn't say." Lewis read on. "And there's not much more to the story of the lamia. Some stories of the Chippewa tell about an owl spirit that lures children away from home and drinks their blood. The writer seems to think that might be tied in to d'Anjou and his magic. Nothing here tells how to kill a lamia. No magic spells or anything."

"Well, from what your uncle told us, we're not dealing with a magic spell here. I wonder if this critter could be what he meant by *deep magic*."

But that was a question neither could answer. Rose Rita found a passage in Mrs. Zimmermann's dissertation that dealt with amulets of summoning. These were magical objects that could call up ghosts or spirits, but none seemed to be whistles. The typed book mentioned Aladdin's lamp and genies and rings that gave the wearer power over spirits, but there was nothing remotely like Lewis's discovery. Finally a yawning Rose Rita shut the dissertation with a clap. The big clock on the upstairs landing bonged dolefully ten times. It was getting late.

"Uncle Jonathan will be back any minute now," said Lewis. "We'd better put the books up."

Rose Rita stretched. "All right. I think I can keep track of how Stan and Billy are doing in the hospital. Your job is to get rid of that whistle if it shows up again. Give it to Mrs. Zimmermann. If anybody can deal with it, she can."

Lewis nodded. It wasn't that easy, but he could think of nothing to say that would convince Rose Rita of the fact. And so he kept quiet.

That night Lewis took Mrs. Zimmermann's dissertation up to his room. He told himself that it was possible Rose Rita had missed something. He lay propped up in bed and turned the pages, reading all about the Philosopher's Stone and the Ring of Solomon and the Seal of the Pharaohs. Nothing. Then as he looked through the footnotes, he noticed one that rang a faint bell: "For further information on amulets of summoning, see Girardus Abucejo, *From the Vasty Deep*." Lewis closed the bound typescript and frowned in thought. Abucejo was an unusual name, and he thought he had seen it before. Maybe Uncle Jonathan had that very book in his study.

Quietly, Lewis slipped out of bed. He opened his bedroom door and heard the faint, muffled sounds of Jonathan Barnavelt's snores. Still barefoot, Lewis tiptoed down the back stairway. He glanced up at the magic window, a stained-glass oval that Uncle Jonathan kept enchanted so that it was always changing. Tonight it showed a tall wizard standing in front of a strange arched bridge, with stone sculptures like giant chess pieces at its corners. The magician was flinging a handful of playing cards through the air toward the bridge.

Lewis padded to the bottom of the stairs and switched on the light. He went to the study and replaced Mrs. Zimmermann's dissertation on its shelf, then began to run his finger across the names on the spines of the other volumes. Aansen, Abbott, Abson, ah, yes: Abucejo. Lewis pulled the volume from the shelf. It was old, with brown pages and a crumbling cloth binding. The title and author's name had been stamped on in gilt, but most of the gold color had flaked away, leaving just the outline of the letters. Lewis sat at the desk and turned on the green-shaded light again. He opened the book and read the title page:

FROM THE VASTY DEEP

By Girardus Abucejo, MMRS

"I can call spirits from the vasty deep."
—Wm. Shakespeare

London: Malleficus Press, 1888

Hurriedly, Lewis turned to the table of contents. It had not only the chapter titles, but a summary of the chapter contents too:

Lewis scanned through these until he came to Chapter 8, which was about "Dangers of attempting to control spirits. Spirit possession. Entrapment of the will." His heart felt as if it had climbed up into his throat and were pounding away behind his Adam's apple. Lewis gulped a couple of times and turned to page 133, where the chapter began. His eyes were watering. He blinked and started to read. He came to a chilling passage:

> . . . but the chief worry of the magician bold enough to conjure up such a spirit is the simple principle of *quid pro quo.* Ancient authorities all agree that such magic must be paid for. Payment may take many forms, some of the most common being the gift of blood (for spirits are always desirous of having a physical body, and the blood of the living is one way of forming such a body), or of obedience, or even an exchange of life for life.
>
> This last is the most terrible. The hapless magician discovers himself locked outside his own body, whilst some loathsome spirit enters it and takes control. In such cases, payment is indeed complete, for the servant spirit has now become, to the world's sight, the magician, and the magician has become

what the spirit was, bodiless and lost upon the wind,
lost for all of time and all of eternity.

Lewis's head spun. He jumped up from the desk and
hurriedly replaced the book on its shelf. Payment? For
blowing a whistle? Could it be true?

He turned out the light and was just going into the hall
when something made him look back. Behind the desk
was a set of French doors that led into the side yard.
These were always closed, and gauzy white curtains hung
over them. The curtains stirred as if in a breeze, though
Lewis could feel no wind.

He wanted to slam the door closed, to dash upstairs
and throw himself in bed. He wanted to hide under the
covers, to feel safe in his room.

But his muscles refused to move. The curtains billowed, rising in the air. He could glimpse the darkness
of the yard beyond them, with patches of drifting night
mist curling and writhing against the glass. The curtains moved again. They rose, fell, hid the closed French
doors, then revealed them.

Someone was standing in the yard.

Come to me.

Lewis gasped. Was that a voice? Or was it only words
he heard in his head? It was the same sensation he had felt
when the ghost had declared that Stan was *Mine*, the
same whispery sense that he had experienced when the
thought of *Revenge* had come into his head. An imaginary
voice, he had told himself over and over. Now he desperately wanted to believe he was imagining things.

The curtains lifted on the unfelt breeze. A woman stood just outside the house. She was white, as pale as moonlight, tall and slender. *Come to me.* Was she speaking to Lewis? Was it her voice he heard in his head? He couldn't be sure. He felt odd, as if he were asleep and awake at the same time.

The woman wore robes that billowed around her just as the curtains billowed in the room. Her face was beautiful and cold, her hair indistinct and dark.

But her eyes—

Her eyes were empty pits.

She stretched out her hands.

Lewis saw her lips form his name. And she smiled. And a moment later the voice said, *Lewis. You must open the doors.*

Her smile pierced Lewis as if it had been a dagger.

He saw his hands rise. Saw them fumble at the latch and push against the doors.

Without a sound, the French doors opened.

She looked wrong. She looked as if her body were formed of the night mists, almost transparent, wavering on the night air. She spread her arms, reaching for him. *We will belong to each other. Together we will be strong. Come to me.*

Lewis tried to say "No," but he could not open his mouth. He was freezing and burning all at the same time. He felt himself take one unwilling step toward the woman . . .

And then all was darkness.

*　　*　　*

When he woke the next morning, Lewis lay in his own bed. He leaped up as if something had stung him. For a moment he stood beside the bed swaying.

He remembered—what?

"It was a dream," he told himself. "It was just a dream."

But was it?

CHAPTER EIGHT

Over the next few days, Lewis felt stranger and stranger. It still wasn't that he was sick, exactly, but he was not himself. Rose Rita noticed it on Friday, when she came over to tell him that she had heard both Billy and Stan were being moved to a bigger hospital in Detroit, miles and miles away. "The doctors think they have some kind of unusual anemia," she told Lewis. "They pump them full of blood about every other day, and then it just seems to disappear somehow."

"Umm," said Lewis, preoccupied. They were sitting in the backyard of Lewis's house again. The sun was bright and hot, but Lewis hardly felt it. To him it seemed as if the world were in a hazy fog, and as if he were somehow not part of it.

Rose Rita squinted at him. "Are you okay? You're not getting sick too, are you?"

"No," replied Lewis. "Just tired, I think. I keep having these crazy dreams, and it's hard to sleep at night."

"You need some vitamins or something," pronounced Rose Rita. "My mom would say you look peaked. Has that whistle showed up again?"

"Haven't seen it."

"If it does, remember—grab it, hold on to it, and give it to Mrs. Zimmermann or your uncle."

Lewis made a face. "You've only told me about a hundred times!" It was odd, but he had never much noticed how bossy Rose Rita always was. He began to think he might be better off without her as a friend. Always sticking her nose into his business, always thinking she knew what was best for everyone. He was getting fed up with her pushy nature.

Now she gave him an anxious, searching look. "Really, Lewis, maybe you should tell your uncle you're feeling sick. He could let Doc Humphries check you out."

"I'm *not* sick!" snapped Lewis. "I'm just tired, that's all."

"Well, excuse me all to pieces," said Rose Rita coldly. "I'm sorry, Your Majesty. I just thought you might want to know about Billy and Stan—"

"I hope Billy and Stan die," said Lewis spitefully.

Rose Rita's eyes opened wide in shock. "Lewis!"

"Always picking on me," grumbled Lewis. "Always calling me names and planning to beat me up. I think it serves them right to land in the hospital! And I'll bet there are a lot of others who think the same thing too!"

Now Rose Rita was blushing, but with anger, not embarrassment. "Be careful what you say, Lewis. You don't mean that. It's a hateful thing to say, and anyway, you'll have to confess all that to Father Foley!"

"He's another one who should be in the hospital," growled Lewis. "Thinks he's so great just because he's a priest! But he's mean, and he loves pushing people around. He needs a taste of his own medicine—"

Rose Rita leaped up from the lawn chair where she'd been sitting. "I'm going home!"

Lewis glared at her. "Good!"

Rose Rita took a few steps, then turned, with her hands on her hips. "And maybe I won't come back until you get in a better mood!"

"Stay away, then!" yelled Lewis after her.

When she had gone, he just sat there for a while, breathing hard. He felt strange. Sad, but sad as if he were remembering how it felt. Mostly he just felt exhausted, tired of everything. He closed his eyes and imagined he heard a song, a wordless humming sort of song, rising and falling as softly as the summer wind. He opened his eyes a moment later to find that shadows had stretched out long across the lawn. Lewis jumped up, alarmed. Hours had gone past as if they had been seconds. He shook his head in confusion. Then he hurried inside.

Mrs. Zimmermann came over that evening for dinner. They had a lot of Lewis's favorites: grilled trout and fresh corn on the cob, dripping with butter, sweet green peas that popped when you bit into them, and fresh-baked bread. Lewis ate mechanically, and to him it all tasted like cardboard.

"Well," boomed Uncle Jonathan as they got to the end of their meal, "Helen called this afternoon and wanted to know why I haven't seen her in so long. So I suppose I'll have to pack up the old buggy and drive out to Ossee Five Hills tomorrow. Want to come, Lewis?"

Lewis didn't. He didn't much like visiting his uncle Jimmy and his aunt Helen, and usually he wormed out of going more than a few times every year. But just the thought of staying behind, all alone in the big empty house, suddenly made him feel shaky and afraid. "Sure," he said.

Uncle Jonathan looked at him in some surprise. "All right. We'll try not to stay too long."

It seemed to Lewis that Mrs. Zimmermann's expression was suspicious. He sighed and said, "Maybe if I go now, I won't have to go again until Christmas." Then, trying to make his voice sound normal, he stood up and said, "I'll wash if you'll dry."

"I'll dry," said Mrs. Zimmermann.

They stood at the sink, with Lewis scrubbing the dishes and Mrs. Zimmermann drying and putting them away. She had cooked for Lewis and Jonathan so often that she knew very well where everything went. At first they were silent, but then Mrs. Zimmermann asked, "Is there anything you need to get off your chest, Lewis?"

He shook his head and handed her a clean pot.

With a sigh, Mrs. Zimmermann said, "I hope this isn't

about the grave in the woods, if grave it was. I'm still trying to learn something about that. In fact, I've asked for a rare book to be sent to me so I can read up on it. It should be here before very long, so maybe then—"

"I wish you wouldn't bother," said Lewis.

Mrs. Zimmermann grinned at him. "Not a chance, kemosabe! You got my curiosity up, and it's like an itch I can't reach, let alone scratch. Just for my own nosiness, I have to see if I can find out about the *lamia* that *jacets hic.* Lord, my old Latin teacher would be scandalized to hear me say that!" She chattered on.

Lewis felt grumpier and grumpier. He could tell that she was trying to humor him, and he resented it. After they had finished with the dishes, all three of them sat in the study. Jonathan broke out the blue-and-gold Capharnaum County Magicians Society playing cards and the one-franc pieces he used as poker chips and suggested a few hands of Siberian Tiger, a fiendishly complicated game that Lewis usually enjoyed. That night, though, Lewis couldn't keep his mind on the cards, and soon he threw his last hand in and announced he was going to bed. He left Uncle Jonathan and Mrs. Zimmermann still playing as he trudged upstairs. "I wish everybody would leave me alone," he grumbled to himself as he turned in. "Treat me like . . . like . . ." But he had already fallen asleep, almost the moment his head touched the pillow.

The next day Uncle Jonathan woke Lewis up bright and early, and they went out and piled into the 1935 Muggins Simoon. It had a starter on the floor that you had to press with your foot as you turned the key in the ignition. For a long time the motor ground on with an *R-r-rrR-rrr* sound until finally the engine coughed, turned over, and then chugged along steadily. "I think the battery's going," said Uncle Jonathan. "I'll have to buy a new one next week."

Lewis didn't say anything, but he thought it was just like Uncle Jonathan to put off things like that. Jonathan Barnavelt was lazy, that's what he was. He never wanted to do chores until he had to, and then if he could postpone them a little longer, he'd do it. Lewis rested his chin on his hand as they drove along toward the little town of Ossee Five Hills, watching the cornfields and small farms roll past. People out working in their fields or their yards pointed and laughed and waved as the boxy old car went past.

That was another thing. Why didn't Uncle Jonathan get rid of this clunky old antique car and get a new one? Even Mrs. Zimmermann drove a better car than this, a purple Plymouth that she had named Bessie. It was a few years old, but it wasn't as ancient as this decaying heap.

Lost in his gloomy thoughts, Lewis rode silently beside his uncle until they reached Ossee Five Hills and then drove a little past it to the white frame house where Jonathan's sister Helen and her husband, Jimmy, lived. With a sigh, Lewis climbed out of the car and followed his uncle to the house.

Aunt Helen had the personality of a leaky inner tube. Unlike her older brother, she was thin and nervous-looking. Instead of Uncle Jonathan's coppery red thatch, she had mousy brown hair. She greeted them sniffily at the door and had them sit in the parlor. Lewis knew he had to sit absolutely still and not swing his feet or say anything unless he was spoken to. Aunt Helen didn't much approve of boys anyway, and especially not of Lewis. Uncle Jimmy was a Baptist, and she had become a Baptist too, when she married him, and more than once she'd hinted to Uncle Jonathan that she would have been happier if he were not trying to raise Lewis as a Catholic. She had been to a Catholic school herself as a girl, but she had hated it.

"James will be here soon," said Aunt Helen. "We will all have lunch. I've prepared some watercress sandwiches and some spinach and tomato soup."

"That's fine, Helen," said Uncle Jonathan, hiding a grimace. "How are you feeling these days?"

Aunt Helen dramatically placed a hand on her thin chest. "You would not believe, Jonathan, how I suffer from asthma. I say it's all these atomic tests the government is doing out in Nevada. I'm sure that horrible fallout drifts right up here to Michigan, and it's making everyone sick. I was reading in the paper just the other day about those mysterious cases of anemia you have down in New Zebedee. It's atomic sickness, you mark my words!"

Lewis sighed. His aunt was a little nutty on the subject of atomic bombs. And she went on and on. She detailed all her symptoms and kept insisting that Jonathan and Lewis could have no idea of how much she suffered. Lewis thought he was suffering a good deal himself, but he didn't dare say anything. After an hour or so, the front door banged and Uncle Jimmy came in. He was a skinny, balding man whose expression was usually weary and long-suffering. Lewis could understand that. Anyone married to Aunt Helen would become tired before long, and he would have to suffer a lot!

Lewis didn't care much for the thin soup or the sandwiches, and after lunch, when Uncle Jonathan stretched and said how nice the visit had been, he was relieved. They went out and climbed into the car, and Jonathan turned to Helen and Jimmy, who had followed them out. "Nice to see you both," said Uncle Jonathan. "You'll have to come to New Zebedee and visit us one of these times."

Aunt Helen put her hand to her chest again and gasped weakly. "I'm afraid I'm not up to a long trip," she said in a weepy voice.

"Well, so long, all," replied Jonathan. He turned the key and stepped on the starter. From beneath the hood came a discouraged sort of clunk, but that was all.

He tried again, and did not even get the clunk. "Battery," said Uncle Jimmy, opening up the folding hood of the old car.

"James, don't you dare get all filthy with motor oil," warned Aunt Helen. "Those are perfectly good clothes you're wearing."

"Try it again, Jonathan," said Uncle Jimmy, ignoring her, as he wiggled something under the hood.

Jonathan turned the key and stepped on the starter. The car gave out a pathetic little whining sound.

"Dead as a doornail," said Uncle Jimmy. "No doubt about it. Well, I can run you into town and we'll see if we can scare up a battery. Though this one's not standard, you know."

"I know," said Uncle Jonathan, climbing out of the car. "I have the people down at the Bass Garage in New Zebedee keep one in stock for me, but they're hard to find."

They parked Lewis back in the parlor, where he sat and leafed through some of his aunt's boring magazines, all about how to grow flowers and how to arrange furniture. Hours passed. By the time Uncle Jimmy's Chevrolet rolled back into the yard, it was dark outside. For another half hour the two men tinkered with the Muggins Simoon, until at last it started. Then they came inside, oily and dirty, to the horror of Aunt Helen.

"We'd better get on the road," said Uncle Jonathan as soon as he had cleaned up.

"You will do no such thing," scolded Aunt Helen. "Why, it would be long past midnight before you could get back to New Zebedee! You and Lewis will stay here for the night, and you can get an early start first thing in the morning."

Lewis gave his uncle a despairing look, but it was no use. They had a dismal dinner of fried salmon croquettes, lumpy mashed potatoes, and stringy green beans. Then Uncle Jonathan and Uncle Jimmy listened to a Detroit Tigers baseball game on the radio. Aunt Helen made up the guest bedroom for Jonathan. She brought an armload of sheets and a flat pillow into the living room. "Lewis, you will have to manage on the sofa," she said with a sigh. "Try not to toss and turn all night! I'm sure it's bad for the springs."

Lewis was seething. When the ball game ended with a Tiger victory, everyone went off to bed. He stripped down to his underclothes and tried to get comfortable on the sofa. That was impossible. The sofa cushions bulged in the wrong places and sagged in the wrong places. Each cushion had a cloth-covered button in its very center, and even through a folded blanket and two sheets, they prodded Lewis in maddening ways. The pillow was almost useless. Even worse, both Aunt Helen and Uncle Jimmy snored, even louder than Uncle Jonathan, and before long the house sounded like a sawmill.

Finally, somehow, Lewis drifted off to sleep. Perhaps because he was sleeping on the lumpy sofa, he dreamed that he was back at the Boy Scout camp near the woods and the flat stone, sleeping on the ground. He did not seem to have a tent or a sleeping bag, though.

In his dream, an owl hooted over and over, each hoot becoming longer and shriller, until they all blended in the sound of a whistle. It pulled him to his feet and made him walk, stiffly, over the meadow. A pale moon was high in the midnight sky, and in its faint light he saw what first looked like a group of boulders. But as he came closer, he realized that one of the shapes was really Stan Peters, lying on his back, and the other was a woman bending over the form of Billy Fox. She rose as Lewis came closer.

He stared dully down. Stan Peters was dead. His face

was as pale as the moonlight, his flesh shrunken like a mummy's. And as Lewis stared, Billy Fox took one gasping breath and then stopped breathing. He was dead too.

"You killed them," said Lewis to the woman.

"To become more real," replied the woman, though her sweet voice was only a whisper in his mind. "Hide their bodies."

"Where?" asked Lewis.

"Beneath my stone."

In the dream Lewis did not protest that he was not strong enough. He tugged at Stan's leg and found that he was as light as a bundle of rags. He grabbed Billy's foot and pulled. Dragging both of them, he walked down the hill.

The stone lay in the clearing, the same three-foot-thick flat boulder he had seen in real life. Lewis dropped Billy's and Stan's feet and tugged at the stone. It swung up as if on hinges, silently. Beneath it yawned a hole. Lewis shoved first Stan's body and then Billy's into the opening. He heard a clatter.

Looking down, Lewis felt a surge of nausea. The hole was perhaps six feet long and four feet wide, like a grave, but it was much deeper. Fifteen or twenty feet down, Billy and Stan had landed on a jumbled pile of bones. Thousands of people must have been buried here!

And to his horror, Lewis saw Billy's eyes slowly open. From Stan's mouth came a horrible moan: "You killed us! You let her drink our blood!"

Lewis slammed the stone down and spun around. The woman stood behind him, the moonlight shining right through her. She was a pale bluish-white, except for her lips.

Her lips were red.

"I need more food," she whispered in his mind. "Perhaps that nosy girl Rose Rita. Or perhaps your aunt. No one would miss her . . ."

Something tugged at Lewis's feet. He looked down. From beneath the stone a tentacle of darkness had crept. It had wrapped itself around both of Lewis's legs. It was pulling, pulling with a terrible force. He knew he could not break away. He knew the shadow would drag him under the rock—

Lewis jumped up from the couch. The dead were screaming! Their cries echoed in his ears!

Then he heard Uncle Jimmy's cranky voice: "Helen, what in the world are you bellowing for?"

Uncle Jonathan came from the guest room and knocked on Uncle Jimmy and Aunt Helen's door. Uncle Jimmy opened it. What little hair he had was frizzed out around his ears. He looked like a daisy that had begun to wilt. "Bad dream," he grunted.

Aunt Helen appeared behind him, rollers in her hair and her face terrified. "The curtains!" she shrieked. "The curtains came to life! They stared at me! Only they didn't have any eyes!"

Past his aunt, Lewis saw the white curtains swaying in a breeze from the half-opened window. Just for an instant, they billowed into the shape of a face, a horrible pitiless face with no eyes, but blank holes where eyes should be. Then it was gone.

"It was just a dream," said Jonathan comfortingly.

But he gave Lewis an uneasy look over his shoulder as he said it.

And despite the shock of having awakened to his aunt's terrified shouts, Lewis smiled a little. "It was just a dream," he said. "That's all it was."

CHAPTER NINE

By the middle of the third week in July, Rose Rita was feeling frantic with worry. She and Lewis had occasionally had tiffs before, as all friends do, but this one seemed to be getting really serious. She had expected him to call and mutter some kind of apology. She was more than willing to forgive him. Days had gone by, however, and she had not heard even one word from him.

Billy and Stan had been in the news again recently. They seemed to be doing better in the hospital in Detroit. Their blood count, whatever that was, had returned to almost normal, and they were able to get out of bed. Still, the doctors did not want to let them leave the hospital. No one could understand what was wrong with them to begin with, and the doctors wanted to find out what had given them such severe anemia in the first place.

They were going to have to have a lot of tests, and doctors in New Zebedee were being asked to report any suspicious or unusual cases with symptoms like theirs.

Every day Rose Rita called Mrs. Zimmermann to ask if she had learned anything else about the grave in Richardson's Woods, or about the whistle. Every day Mrs. Zimmermann's answer was no. She always cautioned Rose Rita not to worry herself too much, but that was like cautioning a fish not to swim. Rose Rita just couldn't help worrying. Finally, able to stand the suspense no more, Rose Rita rode her bike over to High Street, but not to visit Lewis. She went straight to Mrs. Zimmermann's house.

Mrs. Zimmermann let her in, and the two of them sat in her kitchen, munching gooey chocolate chip cookies and drinking milk. "He's turned weird," complained Rose Rita.

"Lewis, you mean?" asked Mrs. Zimmermann, her eyes twinkling behind her spectacles.

Rose Rita nodded. "I know he's worried about that whistle and the stone in the woods. He thinks he's set free some kind of ghost. I understand all that. But I'm on his side. He didn't have any reason to bite my head off."

Mrs. Zimmermann sighed. "Well, sometimes we have to make an allowance or three, Rose Rita. I know you only mean to help Lewis, but there are times when the menfolk think they don't need any help. They are almost always wrong, of course, but that doesn't keep their silly male pride from getting dented when we women dash in, all flags flying, to take charge and set things right."

"It wasn't like that!" But Rose Rita twisted in her chair with the uncomfortable feeling that, yes, it was at least a *little* like that. She stared glumly at the table. A white tablecloth with embroidered violets in a bright shade of purple covered it. She rubbed her finger over one bumpy violet. "Back when Lewis had that magician's amulet that lured him off into the wilderness, *you* came to the rescue!"

Mrs. Zimmermann shivered. "Ugh. Yes, indeed, and a fat lot of good it did! That evil ghost was so strong that when I tried a spell on it, it drained away all my magic power for a couple of years! Much more, and I think it would have killed me. And even so, I wasn't the only reason it lost the fight, as you well know. Lewis had a lot to do with that himself."

"But we helped him!" insisted Rose Rita.

Mrs. Zimmermann gave her a wrinkly smile. "And we will help him again! But you can't just go jumping onto your horse and riding madly off in all directions at once, you know. Believe me, Rose Rita, I have been trying to learn about *lamiae* and even silver whistles, but all I've turned up is such a deal of skimble-skamble stuff that it makes my head ache! The history of real magic is all tangled up with folklore, fairy tales, and just plain lies. It's hard to find a needle of truth in such a messy haystack of ignorance!"

Rose Rita stopped picking at the embroidery on the tablecloth and took a bite from a cookie. "But I hate just doing nothing! Has the book you sent for come?"

Mrs. Zimmermann patted Rose Rita's free hand. "Not

yet, but I know it has been shipped. I expect it tomorrow or the next day."

Rose Rita put down her half-eaten cookie. "Well, in the meantime, is there anything Lewis can do to make himself safe?"

"I don't know for sure," said Mrs. Zimmermann slowly, thoughtfully touching her forefinger to her chin. "I'd say the main thing was not to blow that blamed whistle if he should come across it again. Some magical amulets don't work on the first try. They gain power gradually as the owner tries them out. You know the old saying, 'Third time's a charm'? Sometimes that's literally true."

"I'm going to go right over there and warn him," said Rose Rita. "I don't care if he does think I'm meddling in things I shouldn't. I think he's a—a stubborn pig-headed donkey!"

Mrs. Zimmermann chuckled. "Heavens, Rose Rita! You have quite a way with words. But if Lewis is still brooding, be understanding. I'm sure that he's worried about those scouting friends of his who are in the hospital."

Rose Rita's mouth opened in surprise. "You know about Billy and Stan?"

"I do indeed," replied Mrs. Zimmermann tartly. "I don't live in Outer Mongolia, you know! And I know that those two are bullies and that they take a particular delight in pushing poor Lewis around. Whatever is wrong with them, I'm sure Lewis feels guilty about it. He's just the sort to think he's behind all the woes of his friends and his enemies, like Joe Bfstplk!"

Despite her feelings, Rose Rita had to smile at that. In

a newspaper comic strip called "Li'l Abner," Joe Bfstplk—and how Mrs. Zimmermann had managed to pronounce that name, she could not say—was a lumpy, chinless little guy who was the world's worst jinx. He walked around with a dark cloud over his head. He was always trying to help his friends, and always his best efforts caused some kind of calamity. "But Lewis isn't like that," objected Rose Rita. "Not really."

"That doesn't keep him from feeling sometimes that he causes trouble or that the whole world is against him," pointed out Mrs. Zimmermann. "You've had days like that, Rose Rita. I've had days like that. Everyone has. The trouble with Lewis is that he thinks it's just him. Maybe the best thing a good friend could do is just be ready when he needs her. 'They also serve who only stand and wait,' as John Milton said."

That really wasn't enough to satisfy Rose Rita. When she saw Jonathan Barnavelt come out of his house a few minutes later, she hurriedly said good-bye to Mrs. Zimmermann and rushed out to catch up with him. She did, about halfway down the street. He greeted her with some surprise. "What's cooking, Rose Rita? I haven't seen you for days. You look all done in."

Rose Rita shrugged. "I'm okay. I came over to ask about Lewis. I haven't heard from him in a while."

Jonathan stroked his beard. "Hardly anyone has," he muttered. "He's been grouchy and cranky and snappy lately. In fact, if those three were all members of the Seven Dwarfs, Lewis could be any one of them!"

"Is he doing okay?"

They walked along side by side. "He's turned into a hermit," said Jonathan slowly. "He comes out of his room for meals, but except for that, he hardly says three words a day to me. I think he's still really worried about that stone out in Richardson's Woods, and about the whistle he found and then lost."

"He thinks he caused a couple of the Scouts to get sick," explained Rose Rita. She rapidly filled him in on what had happened to Billy and Stan as they walked toward town.

When she finished, Jonathan looked serious. "Thank you for telling me the whole story. Florence and I have talked about Billy and Stan, of course. But I've never heard of a magic whistle that could summon up an illness, and neither has she. Our feeling is that it's probably just a coincidence that the two of them got sick. They pal around together, and if one of them caught some kind of germ, the other probably would get it too. I don't know. This doesn't seem like magic, but that's something that Florence and I will keep in mind. Still, it's something that Lewis would worry about, all right. It's just like him to take something like this to heart," he observed.

"Then you don't think the whistle had anything to do with Billy and Stan getting sick?"

Jonathan answered her with quiet assurance: "Strolling along here in broad daylight, no. But then, I'm a fuddy-duddy grown-up, and if I were Lewis's age, and half afraid of my own shadow, or if it were a dark, dark night—well, that might be another story! Do you remember a few years ago when there was that polio scare?"

Rose Rita did. It was the year she was eight. A kid came down with a case of polio, and everyone in New Zebedee had panicked. The Athletic Field had closed, and lots of families had left town. Fortunately, the victim had not had a serious case, and he had almost completely recovered, and happily Dr. Jonas Salk had come up with a vaccination that kept people from getting polio these days. Still Rose Rita recalled how frightened and worried her mother had been. "I remember all about it," she told Jonathan.

"Well, Lewis found an old newspaper with that story in it the year he came to live with me," Jonathan went on. "My gosh, how that boy fretted! Every little ache or itch or tickle meant he was coming down with polio, and he actually hid from me one day to keep me from catching it! Lewis has what you might call an overdeveloped organ of guilt. That's one reason I'd like Father Foley to ease up on him a little. Lewis gets himself into a stew over every little thing, and he's such a worrier that the slightest little problem sometimes flummoxes him. And then something very serious comes along and that just about pushes him over the edge. I'm glad he has a friend like you, Rose Rita."

She blushed a little. "I wish he'd let me help more," she muttered.

Jonathan nodded, and then smiled. It looked to Rose Rita as if he were trying to force himself to be cheerful again. "Well, I'm off to the barber shop, Rose Rita. I'd suggest you pay a call on old grouchy-cranky-snappy, but he's probably still not in the mood for company. Don't worry. These things blow over, you know."

"I hope so," said Rose Rita.

*   *   *

In the mansion at 100 High Street, Lewis Barnavelt had seen all of this. He had been standing at a front window when Rose Rita ran past the house, and from another window, he saw her catch up to his uncle and walk off talking to him. He felt a dull anger. Here she was again, poking her nose into business that didn't concern her! He clenched and unclenched his fists. Why, if he had the whistle—

With a groan, Lewis pressed his hand over his eyes. "I didn't mean that," he said, not knowing if anyone or anything could hear him. "I don't want anything to happen to Rose Rita."

But she is not important.

Lewis almost yelped, and he actually jumped in his surprise and fright. He heard the voice very often now, a woman's voice, but somehow it always came from inside his head. "She's my friend."

I am your friend. I am hungry.

Lewis did not say anything. What was the voice suggesting? That he should somehow give Rose Rita to—to the thing that had attacked Billy and Stan?

The stone is very heavy. The stone holds me down. I cannot go far unless I am called. The others are too far, too far away.

"B-Billy and Stan?" asked Lewis.

The voice, or whatever it was, did not bother to reply. Lewis had heard about people losing their minds and hearing voices that no one else could hear. Was that happening to him? What if he wound up sitting in a padded cell, wrapped in a straitjacket, drooling and gibbering and talking to someone who wasn't even real?

"Where's the whistle?" he asked. He had asked that same question dozens of times now.

No answer came.

Lewis wandered through the house restlessly. In the front hall, he looked into the magic mirror on the hat stand. Instead of reflecting his face, it showed some strange stone coffins, with hollows scooped out in them for the bodies. They lay scattered about a pebbly yard. It had appeared before, and Uncle Jonathan had told him the coffins were in Holyrood Abbey in Scotland, where Mary, Queen of Scots, had once lived. After England had broken away from the Roman Catholic church, King Henry VIII had closed all the abbeys in 1537, and looters had emptied the tombs, seeking jewelry.

Lewis stared at one of the stone coffins. It had been chiseled out so that the interior had a hollow shaped somewhat like a mummy: The legs broadened toward the hips, and then there was a rounded niche for the chest and shoulders, and a smaller oval one for the head. Lewis could just imagine what it might feel like to be pushed into one of those, to see the heavy stone lid slide into place, shutting out the light—

He felt as if he were going to have a nervous break-down. He could not read, he could not concentrate on television or radio, he didn't feel like talking to anyone. It was a bit like being shut up in a coffin at that, he thought bitterly.

"I want—I want—" he murmured. He wanted what?

"I want my life back," he said in a hopeless whisper.

I want life.

Lewis clapped his hands over his ears, although he knew he could not keep that voice out. He climbed the stairs to the bathroom. He stood in front of the medicine chest and unbuttoned his shirt. Fearfully, he pulled it open.

For days he had had two red marks on his chest. They looked like wounds, but they never seemed to heal. He could not remember hurting himself. Or had he? The marks didn't hurt, exactly. They ached, with a low, dull sensation that was not quite pain and not quite an itch. He had swabbed them with Mercurochrome and with hydrogen peroxide, and he had covered them with Band-Aids, but they did not close up or scab over.

What had happened the night he saw the ghostly figure outside the French doors? He could remember nothing after stepping through the door and looking into her terrible empty eyes. Had she lured him outside, or even worse, had she come into the house? Had she—he shuddered—drunk his blood?

He went to his bedroom and pulled open the drawer in his night table. Rummaging in the clutter, he found his mother's rosary and pulled it out. It wasn't fancy. It was just a small silver crucifix hanging from a short length of five white beads. This was attached to a necklace made of five sets of one large coral bead and ten smaller white ones. You were supposed to use the rosary to keep count of your prayers. You could also "pray the rosary," saying prayers like the Apostles' Creed, the Our Father, and the Hail Mary as you counted off the beads.

With his heart going like a hammer, Lewis began with the crucifix: "*In nomine Patris, et Fili, et Spiritus Sancta . . .*"

Red pain rose in his head, blinding him. He fell to his knees and dropped the rosary. For a little while, everything went dark. When he could see again, he found himself lying crumpled on the floor and clutching his head, as if to keep it from exploding. Tears were running from both of his eyes.

Put that . . . thing away. You will not need it.

Shaking and fearful, Lewis dropped the rosary back into the drawer. He fell facedown on the bed. What was happening to him? What had that figure at the window done to him?

Was he simply going insane?

CHAPTER TEN

Snakelike, eyeless creatures haunted Lewis's dreams. Uncle Jonathan and Mrs. Zimmermann conferred about him, and he was sure that the two of them cast protective spells on the Barnavelt house. Nothing seemed to help. He spent his nights half in terrified sleep and half awake, sweating and shaking, afraid to try to drift off again. He had the strangest sensation of *fading*. Color slowly drained from the world. Sounds came from far distances. When he lay in bed, he could not really feel the mattress beneath him or the sheets on top of him. It was as if he were floating in outer space.

He began to feel a dull anger toward his uncle, Mrs. Zimmermann, and Rose Rita. If they liked him so much, why didn't they help him? And if the whistle was so bad, why was it the only thing that could help him when the chips were down and he faced being beaten to a pulp? More and more Lewis just wanted to be alone.

One Sunday he felt too ill to go to Mass. His uncle stayed home with him, and all that day Lewis remained in bed, complaining of a headache. "If that doesn't clear up by morning, you are going to be checked out by Dr. Humphries," pronounced Jonathan firmly. "This is the first time since you fell off your bike and clonked your noggin that you've had that kind of a headache, and I don't like it."

"I'm not crazy about it myself," growled Lewis, his teeth clamped to hold a thermometer in place.

His uncle hesitated, then patted Lewis's shoulder. "I know you're not. I'm sorry, Lewis. I wasn't hinting that you're pretending. Here, open up." He took the thermometer, squinted at it, and turned it this way and that, peering hard. "Ninety-eight point six," he reported. "You're a normal Norman, as far as your temperature goes." He shook the thermometer. "Feel like any dinner?"

Lewis shook his head.

"Ice cream? Cake? Sauerkraut with chocolate-covered peanuts? A mustard-filled doughnut?"

Lewis groaned. "I just want to rest, that's all."

"Right you are. I'll check in on you a little later," replied Jonathan cheerfully. He went out, closing Lewis's bedroom door behind him.

Lewis twisted in bed and pounded his pillow. Why did his uncle have to tell all those corny jokes, anyway? And what was the big deal in having a touch of headache? All he wanted was to be left alone.

Alone.

But you are never alone, came the soft voice in his head.

"Go away," said Lewis harshly.

The voice spoke no more. But Lewis had the terrible sensation that it was singing, wordlessly, so softly, he could not even be sure he heard the sound. It became stronger when he tried to fall asleep, a hypnotic rise and fall of music at the very edge of his hearing. That made his heart jerk with alarm and woke him up again, over and over.

Daylight faded away from the window. At last, from sheer exhaustion, Lewis did manage to fall into a kind of sleep, or at least unconsciousness. How long he was in that state he could never tell, but at some point something woke him. He had felt a wave of darkness pass over him. It was a flash of black lightning. It was as though he had been touched by the hand of Death.

Lewis sat up in bed. It was the middle of the night, and no light showed in his room, yet he could see. Everything stood out clearly, in shades of dull gray. *You have to go downstairs. Quietly.*

Lewis rolled out of bed. He could barely feel the floor beneath his feet. He had trouble grasping the doorknob. When he closed his hand on it, he felt almost no pressure to tell him he was holding it. He turned it with great difficulty.

Something told him to tiptoe down the back stairs. The oval, changing window was oddly blank and black. It always showed a picture of some sort, but not tonight.

Tonight it was like a window into outer space, out beyond the farthest star.

Before he reached the foot of the stairs, Lewis heard the murmur of voices: his uncle's and Mrs. Zimmermann's. He understood that something wanted him to listen. Something was using his ears to learn what the two of them were talking about. Carefully, he tiptoed to the kitchen door, which stood barely ajar. A thin wedge of light spilled from it. Avoiding this, Lewis put his ear close to the opening. He heard his uncle's voice clearly first: ". . . no fever, but he's complaining about a headache, and he just doesn't look right."

"The volume I've been waiting for will be here tomorrow," replied Mrs. Zimmermann. "At long last! Until then, I suppose we can try all the old folk preventions. Garlic and hawthorn, crucifixes and holy water."

"I have all those," said Uncle Jonathan. "And don't think it was easy to get up the nerve to ask Father Foley for a bottle of holy water, and then for a special blessing on top of it! The man must think I've lost what few marbles I possess. But what was the news you had to run over to tell me, Florence? Nothing else terrible, I hope."

Mrs. Zimmermann was so quiet for so long that Lewis leaned closer to the kitchen door, thinking that she might be whispering. But at last she spoke, in a low but understandable voice: "Billy Fox was released from the hospital yesterday, but his parents are not bringing him back to New Zebedee. They're taking him somewhere out east to live. They blame the town for what happened to him, as if it were some kind of plague spot. But that isn't the worst. The other boy, Stanley Peters . . ."

When she did not go on, Uncle Jonathan said peevishly, "Confound it, Pruny Face, don't leave me hanging! Come on and spill it. I'm a great big man, and I can take it, whatever it is. Did he die?"

"N-nooo," said Mrs. Zimmermann slowly. "He . . . escaped."

"Escaped? Escaped from what? Escaped from who? Did that hospital have bars on the doors and men in uniform patrolling the halls?"

"You mean *from whom*," said Mrs. Zimmermann, who had been a teacher and who hated to hear faulty grammar. "But I don't mean *escaped*, exactly. He slipped out of the hospital two nights ago, taking the clothes he had been wearing when he was admitted. No one has seen him since, and no one knows where he may be headed."

"I can guess," muttered Jonathan. "He's heading back to little old New Zebedee. He's coming home."

Upstairs. Quickly. The command in Lewis's head seemed louder than the voices he had been eavesdropping on, though he knew that no one else could possibly hear them. Quietly but quickly, he climbed the stairs and returned to his own room. *It is too soon, but we have to go now.*

Lewis did not understand. Something ordered him to dress hurriedly, ordered him without even the silent words that he heard only in his head. He didn't have to turn on the light to do so. He could still see in the dark, although everything was lifeless and colorless. He sat in the chair at his desk to tie his shoes, and when he had finished and straightened up, he was not surprised to see the shape of a body beneath the sheet on his bed.

It moved. The sheet clung to the form. What lay beneath the sheet Lewis could not say. Somehow the sheet itself became the body of a woman, the face made of crumpled, wrinkled linen. The mouth was wide and cruel, the nose broad, and the eyes only empty hollows under a projecting brow. The form sat up and rose from the bed. The blind head swiveled and finally faced Lewis. With despair, he saw color again. The empty eye sockets held a deep crimson light that pulsated with the beat of Lewis's heart.

The thing could see.

It reached out a draped arm for him.

Come with me.

And, although some part of his mind was shrieking in terror, Lewis followed the shape.

A little after nine the next morning, the phone rang in the Barnavelt house. Jonathan, who had been sitting at the kitchen table sipping coffee and reading the morning paper, jumped at the sound. He hurried to answer the phone, and as soon as he did, Mrs. Zimmermann's voice buzzed on the line: "Jonathan! Can you come over?"

"What's up?"

Mrs. Zimmermann sounded exasperated: "The book arrived this morning, special delivery. Hurry over and let's see if we can learn what's what. How is Lewis?"

"He hasn't gotten up yet. I looked in on him this morning, and he's lying there under the covers, all huddled up.

I didn't have the heart to wake him, because he's been sleeping so badly. Say, why don't you come over here?"

"Be there in two shakes. Pour an extra cup of coffee, because I think I'll need it." After a pause, she added, "And I'm going to phone Rose Rita and ask her to come over too. I know she's young, but she's been in on this from the start, and I think she deserves to be in on it now." Mrs. Zimmermann hung up with a click, and Jonathan replaced the receiver. He hurried up the stairs and quietly opened Lewis's door. Lewis didn't seem to have moved much. He still lay under the coverlet, huddled up as if he were cold. Carefully, Jonathan closed the door and went back downstairs again.

Mrs. Zimmermann was just opening the kitchen door. She held a book almost twice as tall as an encyclopedia volume against her chest. Behind her glasses, her eyes were sparkling. "Now maybe we'll find out a few things!" She thumped the book down on the table as Jonathan poured her a cup of coffee. He served it to her, and the cream pitcher, which was in the shape of a black-and-white cow, came to life and ambled over to her with a friendly moo. Mrs. Zimmermann made a face as she picked it up and poured a dollop of cream into her coffee from the cow's open mouth. "Please don't hex the sugar bowl," she said to Jonathan. "It makes me feel queasy, having a cow spit cream into my coffee."

Jonathan paid her very little attention because he was studying the mysterious tome. It had a leather cover, pebbly and deep brown, with semiprecious stones set into it in a curly design: black onyxes and purple garnets, blue-green turquoises and yellow citrines, red bloodstones and green jade. He traced these with his index finger. "Someone believes in mineral spells, I see. Whoever made this cover put all the protective stones in just the right order. At least the bookbinder knew his magic!"

"Or hers," returned Mrs. Zimmermann tartly.

Someone knocked on the front door, making them both jump. Jonathan laughed uneasily. "That will be Rose Rita," he said. "She made good time!" He hurried to the foyer and opened the door.

Sure enough, Rose Rita stood on the threshold, looking pale with worry. "What's up?"

"Come with me and you'll see," replied Jonathan. He hastily filled Rose Rita in about the magical book as they walked to the kitchen.

Mrs. Zimmermann greeted Rose Rita. "The more I thought about the word *lamia*, the more certain I was that I had read about it someplace," she explained. "Finally I had the sense to read my own doctoral dissertation again, and that sent me to a book by a man named Abucejo, and *that* directed me to a three-hundred-year-old book that is so rare, I had to pull about a million strings to find a copy. But I have a friend or two in certain European universities, and one of them finally came through. This should tell us about the lamia and how it came to Michigan, if anything can!"

"And how it ties in with Lewis's troubles," agreed Jonathan. "Let's have a look."

Mrs. Zimmermann carefully opened the book. Jonathan craned over her shoulder, squinting at the yellowed parchment. The printing was very old-fashioned, and the language was medieval Latin, but he mentally translated the title:

Of the Lamia

Together with Memoirs of
Fr. Pierre Michel d'Anjou
Rome, 1656
By Fr. Augustus St. Francis Xabier Kemp
Doctor of Philosophy

Mrs. Zimmermann waited impatiently. "You know you're slow as molasses when you're trying to translate in your head! Let me read it to you, translating as I go. That will speed everything up!"

"Go ahead, go ahead," grumbled Jonathan, rolling his eyes. "Just because I got my degree in animal husbandry instead of a fancy-pants doctorate of magic—"

"Oh, quiet, Brush Mush," snapped Mrs. Zimmermann, but in a playful tone, with a wink at Rose Rita. She turned the pages, and then settled down to read. "Hum. All right. Herr Doktor Kemp, it seems, knew Father d'Anjou personally. In fact, when Kemp was a very young man, he was apprenticed to the elderly d'Anjou. D'Anjou was, let's see . . . let's see, not only a priest but also a physician, an explorer, a lawyer, and a magician."

Jonathan snorted. "Oh, peachy. A doctor *and* a lawyer.

After he killed his patients, he could sue himself for malpractice!"

Mrs. Zimmermann didn't even look up from the book. "I know you're just trying to be funny because you're afraid, but that's really quite distracting, so please be quiet for a moment. Let's see . . . yes, in 1611, d'Anjou went along on a voyage of exploration with a party of French adventurers, and the young Kemp was d'Anjou's servant. Voyage over, blah, blah, blah, let's get to the good stuff." Mrs. Zimmermann turned over several pages, her eyes just scanning them. "Aha! Also, Oho! and other expressions of wonderment. Here we are. The group was traveling overland, trading with the native people they encountered. The spelling is outlandish, but I think Kemp is talking about the Ojibway and the Potawatomi. Anyway, listen to this: 'My master kept us all safe, for he had in his possession a silver tube that called a spirit the people of the forest much feared.'"

"Bingo," said Jonathan. "All right, what else?"

"Don't worry your beard white," returned Mrs. Zimmermann. "Uh-oh. According to Kemp, after a time d'Anjou refused to use the whistle, because 'he had twice used it, and to call upon the spirit a third time would cause it to take his life, or the lives of his nearest friends.'"

"Sounds bad," admitted Jonathan. "Let me guess: He used it a third time."

Mrs. Zimmermann was turning pages again. Her face was pale. "Father d'Anjou proposed setting up a mission in what surely must be Michigan today. The French traders with him tricked some of the Potawatomi, and then attacked them. They killed several, but some got away. They returned with a war party and soon eleven of the thirty-two Frenchmen were dead, and the others were about to be overwhelmed. Father d'Anjou blew the whistle, and something dreadful happened."

Rose Rita squirmed impatiently. "What?"

Mrs. Zimmermann looked up, her eyes sick. "Kemp isn't willing to say. But the attacking Potawatomi warriors were all killed, to the last man. And over the next days, every one of the French explorers died, one after the other. Listen: 'Now it had shape and substance. Now it prowled the forest, beyond my master's control. When but the two of us were left, my master took me to a place where a stone lay in the manner of a tomb. Here we would end it, if anywhere.' Kemp says they drew a magic circle, and 'with holy water, with the holy crucifix, and with other amulets of power, we prepared. And then it came from the forest, in the guise of a creature half serpent, half beautiful woman.' Hmm. Some kind of magical battle. Kemp was almost lost, 'but my master pulled me back within the circle at the last moment.' He took away the creature's body, somehow, and 'like a living shadow, the monster was forced into the holy circle and beneath the stone, where may it lie forever.'"

"Except it didn't," said Jonathan, feeling a wave of nausea. "What about the blasted whistle?"

"Kemp says only that d'Anjou hid it." Mrs. Zimmermann read on. "D'Anjou had made some unholy pact with the servant of the whistle. When its influence was no longer in his life, he began to age unnaturally fast. 'At least a year for every week that passed,' Kemp says. The two of them struggled back to Quebec, which was a new colony at the time. D'Anjou died the day before they arrived there. Kemp says he buried the body on the shore of a river, and then goes on to talk about how he returned to France. He finally finished his education in Wittenberg, and 'never again do I wish to see the deadly shores of New France.'"

"Well, Pruny Face," said Jonathan, "can you whomp up a magic spell as powerful as that of old d'Anjou?"

"I can make a good guess at what he did," replied Mrs. Zimmermann thoughtfully. "The trick will be to make the lamia come out of hiding. For that we need Lewis. I think what must have happened was that the spirit gained control of the blasted whistle somehow or other. D'Anjou was too smart to let that happen while he was alive, but by hook or crook, the lamia arranged to have the whistle found, and used some dire magic to make it appear and disappear just when Lewis was most likely to blow the thing. What we have to do at all costs is to keep him from using it three times."

"Let's get him up," said Jonathan. "Wait for us here, Rose Rita." He held Mrs. Zimmermann's chair as she got up, and the two of them climbed the back stairs of the Barnavelt house. Jonathan tapped lightly on Lewis's door. "Lewis? Time to get up!" He opened the door.

The figure in bed did not move. "Lewis," called Mrs. Zimmermann softly, "we have some news."

"Come on, come on," boomed Jonathan, taking three wide steps into the room. He threw back the blanket that covered Lewis's bed.

Lewis was not under it. His top sheet was gone, and on the mattress lay the crumpled bottom sheet.

"Oh, my Lord!" Mrs. Zimmermann covered her mouth and with her free hand pointed at the blanket, which Jonathan had flung to the floor.

Jonathan gasped in alarm.

The blanket had settled into the shape of a sleeping Lewis, but when Jonathan whipped it away, nothing was beneath it.

The shape under the blanket was some trick of the lamia, some trick to delay them.

And it had worked only too well.

CHAPTER ELEVEN

Jonathan Barnavelt threw open the front door of his house—and ran head-on into a startled-looking Father Foley. "What's happened?" demanded the priest, staggering back a step or two.

Jonathan looked at him, his eyes wild. "Father Foley! I—you've caught me at a bad time, and I can't talk just now. I was just headed out—"

The old priest frowned. "So I see. And your two guests are heading out with you?"

Stammering, Jonathan introduced Mrs. Zimmermann and Rose Rita. "We, uh, have some important business to take care of," he said, his face flushing. "So if you will excuse us—"

Heavily, in a troubled voice, Father Foley muttered,

"You will at least tell me if this business of yours involves a whistle? A silver whistle, with a magic spell on it?"

Jonathan could only stare, his mouth opening and closing. From beside him, Mrs. Zimmermann said tartly, "Oh, stop giving your impression of a flounder out of water. Father Foley, I'm not Catholic, but I'll confess to you this minute that I know a bit about magic and about spells. Yes, you're right about the whistle. But the question is—how did you know? And the bigger question is *what* do you know?"

The priest glanced over his shoulder, but as far as Jonathan could see, High Street was as peaceful as it ever was at eleven on a sunny morning. Father Foley coughed self-consciously. "May we go inside? I know what you are up against. I know of"—he dropped his voice—"the lamia, and of her limitations. For a few hours she is powerless against those who are not already under her spell. Nothing will happen until tomorrow morning."

Mrs. Zimmermann gave Jonathan a short nod, and the four of them trooped back into the study. The priest sighed as he caught sight of the enormous book on the desk. "Ah," he said. "Now there is something I recognize."

Mrs. Zimmermann touched the jeweled cover. "You have read this?"

With a tired smile, the priest said, "More. I wrote it, dear lady."

Jonathan felt as if someone had hit him with a base-ball bat. "You *wrote* it?" he shouted. "How could that be?

Unless you're over three hundred years old, and your name is really Kemp?"

"I am over four hundred years old," said the priest wearily. "And may God pity me, my name is really d'Anjou."

"The book says he died," objected Rose Rita.

Sinking into a chair, Father Foley pressed a hand to his eyes. "Young Kemp died," he murmured. "I buried him and took his name. At that time, I wanted nothing more to do with the name of d'Anjou or with his foolish magical experiments. It seemed no great harm to take Kemp's name, for he had no family. And I expected to die soon anyway. I had expected my great age to fall upon me with the passing of the lamia, just as the book says. But that did not happen, for my spell was not completely successful. The lamia did not perish and was not banished, but survived. And until the lamia is finally defeated, I cannot die. I can only continue to exist."

"I think some explanations are in order," said Jonathan, slipping into his chair behind the desk.

"I agree," said the priest.

"Are there any more lies in the book?" demanded Rose Rita bluntly.

The priest shook his head. "I wanted to leave some record once I realized I would not die. I lacked the courage to face the lamia again myself, but I thought that some more powerful magician might succeed where I feared to try, and so, yes, I wrote the book." He drew a deep breath. "The first part of the book is completely true. I did gain control of the lamia—never mind how—

and I did use an ancient whistle to summon it. Somehow my life force became tied to that thing, which is only half of this world and half of the spirit realm. I fooled myself, thinking that since I was a priest, my belief and my faith would give me power over the monstrous creature. But alas, neither was strong enough! In the crisis, I could only force the thing beneath a great stone and subdue it into a kind of hibernation. I always knew that one day it would stir again. In the years since, I have gone on, aging very slowly, and always tormented with the knowledge that I did not banish the monster. It cannot be banished, not until . . ." He swallowed hard, and then whispered, "Until I am willing to die."

Mrs. Zimmermann asked softly, "And what have you been up to since 1611?"

The priest spread his wrinkled hands. "I have been a wanderer. Months ago, I felt the stirring of the creature. It troubled my dreams, and I knew that it was trying to come from beneath the stone. At that time I was in a monastery in Ireland. As you might expect, in three hundred and forty-odd years, I have had many names and have learned many languages. But I have always followed my vocation as a priest."

"Why did you come back?" asked Rose Rita.

Looking sick, the old man said, "Because I had to. In the last few years, more and more I became aware that the evil spirit was stirring, trying to reach out and draw a victim to free it. An old hand like me knows how to pull a few strings. It was not difficult to have myself assigned to New Zebedee to become pastor of your church."

Uncle Jonathan said, "I didn't think you were really Irish. But I never could place your accent. Look, if the lamia is so dangerous, why didn't you stick around the whole time to guard its resting place?"

Father Foley grimaced. "I lacked the courage! I knew that is what I should have done. But except for forty years in the last century, when I lived in Boston for a time, I had not been back to this country, and certainly not to this part of it. Now, when I needed to find the stone, everything had changed. I had no way of locating the grave. And so I settled in to watch and to wait. My first clue was when your nephew asked me about the Latin verb *sibila*. At first I thought he'd just found it in a book. It means—"

"'Hiss' or 'whistle,' depending," supplied Mrs. Zimmermann.

"Yes," agreed the priest. "And it was engraved on the whistle that I had used to control the lamia. I could not believe that the boy had actually found the whistle, for the lamia seeks out people who are wise in the ways of magic. Surely the boy isn't—"

"No," said Mrs. Zimmermann grimly. "But his friends are."

"Ah," replied Father Foley. "Then you are the creature's real target. It wants to be part of our world, you see. It wants to have a true body, not just a shape formed of whatever is at hand. To do that, it needs a constant supply of blood. And if the blood is that of a wizard, then the creature takes on the wizard's magic. You cannot dream of, you cannot imagine, the evil the thing could do if it has the guise of a human and the power of magic. The poor boy—his blood might keep the thing going. But it would never satisfy its appalling hungers, not really, and in the end, I suspect the lamia would—would do something especially terrible to Lewis. Well, whatever doubts I had about the creature's intervening in Lewis's life ended when Mr. Barnavelt came to me and asked for holy water. I knew then that he meant to combat something evil, and I wondered if he knew what he was up against. It has taken me this long to work up the courage to come to see him. I am dreadfully afraid."

"I know well enough what we're up against. How do we stop it?" demanded Jonathan impatiently.

With misery in his voice, the old priest said, "God help us, I am not sure we can!"

Lewis Barnavelt did not know where he was or even clearly *who* he was. He had vague memories. He had climbed into the back of a farmer's pickup truck and had hidden there while the farmer drove miles into the country. He had slipped out and cut across fields and through spinneys of woods, half walking and half floating, or so he felt.

The woman was there, ahead of him, a gray shape urging him on. He sobbed with weariness, and yet he could not rest. He felt as if his brain were on fire. The whistle had reappeared in his pocket. Now it hung on its chain around his neck, and it weighed a ton, dragging him down toward the earth. Yet he plodded on, putting one foot in front of the other.

A pale dawn had just begun to break when Lewis found himself staggering into the rocky clearing of the grave. The ghostly woman urged him forward with glances and gestures, and he found himself clambering atop the three-foot-thick stone. It was cold under his bare hands, cold and clammy.

You will rest, commanded the harsh voice in his head. *You must live. You must be here for them to seek.*

He could not form words in his mind. He couldn't reply or even think of anything to say. He sank onto the stone and lay there on his back, with his arms crossed on his chest. He had the sense that the spirit hovered somewhere beyond his feet, but he could not be sure. His hands lay on the whistle, and its silver tube felt cold and hard under his palms. His heart thudded slowly in his ears. He fell into a trance—not into sleep, exactly, but into a vague half-awareness. The cold stone pressed against his back. A sun that seemed drained of heat rose and climbed high. A fitful wind gusted, rattling the trees, but he could not feel or hear it.

As the hours dragged by, Lewis sensed that he somehow was regaining a little strength. Not enough to move or even to speak, but at least he could think again. "What will happen?" he asked himself.

As if it could hear his thought—and no doubt it could—the voice within him replied, *I will triumph. The boy whose blood I took is coming to us. When he arrives, I will drain him, and that will give me the body I need to face the magicians.*

Lewis whimpered. Stan, he thought. Stanley Peters was going to die. And the magicians had to be—

Your foolish uncle. And the cunning witch. She is the stronger of the two. She shall be the last to perish. Their magic will make me strong, will let me live, truly live!

It was an agony to force his eyelids apart, but with a tremendous struggle, Lewis did it. Even with his eyes open, Lewis could see almost nothing. It was as if he were lost in a luminous, silvery fog.

"Don't kill them," he thought desperately. "Take me instead."

You! The voice in his mind was mocking. *You do not even know what you are to me. You are only the doorway. My mistake has ever been to deal with those skilled in magic! The answer was so simple . . . to wait, to bide my time, over hundreds of years until a boy came along, a boy who had no power himself but who lived among those who did. Your friends shall perish, and you are the reason for their perishing. But that is well. You hate them.*

If Lewis could have screamed, he would have done so at the top of his lungs. "No! I don't! I don't!"

As if hearing an echo, Lewis recognized his earlier thoughts, recited in a hateful singsong tone by that interior voice: *If they like me so much, why don't they help me? And if the whistle is so bad, why is it the only thing that could help me when the chips are down and somebody wants to beat me to a pulp?*

"I didn't mean it!"

Don't hide your anger, boy. Taste it. It is sweet, like dark, dark honey. Your revenge will come. Rest now! Rest, I command it!

Lewis lay paralyzed and all but blind. At some time, after lying there for hours or for days, as far as he could tell, another thought finally formed itself, a despairing, hopeless thought: *This is what death is like.*

And the voiceless response to that from the thing that had led him here came instantly, lullingly: *Death? You do not have to worry about death. Not you. The others will perish, but not you. You will live eternally. You will live until the end of time.*

Lewis groaned. The soft, relentless words came to him with no trace of humanity in them: *Poor child! You will wish you were dead. But I cannot venture into the world if there is not a spirit to take my place here.*

"I don't understand."

No, for you are no magician. Magic demands balance. If I become part of your world, then something must take my place here, in the bodiless realm of the spirits. We shall be linked, you and I, for all eternity. I will live! I will truly live in the world. And as for you, well, you will wish you were dead, indeed. Often and often! Forever and always you will wish you were dead as you lie there . . .

beneath the stone!

CHAPTER TWELVE

It was past two o'clock. Mrs. Zimmermann sat in Jonathan Barnavelt's chair in his study, bending forward over a crystal ball she had brought over from her house.

Impatiently, Jonathan demanded, "Do you see anything?"

"I'm trying," responded Mrs. Zimmermann. "It's very difficult for some reason."

Father Foley was pacing back and forth behind Jonathan. "That is the lamia," he said in a thin voice. "She is strong enough to interfere with your magic."

"Mrs. Zimmermann is the best there is," said Rose Rita. She was sitting in the armchair in the corner, her arms crossed and a stubborn look on her face. "She can do it!"

Mrs. Zimmermann glanced up with a tired smile.

"Thanks for your high opinion, Rose Rita, but so far, so bad. But I have an idea. I may not be able to zoom in on Lewis, but I'll bet my purple nightie I can spot Stanley Peters. And he's in on this too!" She bent forward again, peering into the depths of the crystal. It shimmered a pale purple, as if it had trapped a little bit of summer heat lightning.

"Hold on," said Mrs. Zimmermann. "Yes, I see him! Here he is. Now let me see where *here* is . . ."

A walking figure had appeared in the crystal. The picture zoomed out, and suddenly the boy was just a speck trudging along beside a highway. Behind him was a bridge, and ahead of him was a white frame church.

"That's Willow Creek Road," Mrs. Zimmermann said. "He's a few miles outside of town, and he hasn't reached the old Methodist church yet."

"Let's go," said Jonathan. "Prunella, grab your crystal ball and your wand. I've got mine!" He brandished a walking stick with a crystal knob. "Father Foley, get your book. We'll need all the help we can get."

"I'm coming too," announced Rose Rita.

They all piled into Jonathan's Muggins Simoon, and they roared away from the curb, heading east of town. Willow Creek Road was a country byway, and they whizzed past fields of corn and isolated farmhouses. "There he is!" yelled Rose Rita, who was squished between Jonathan and Mrs. Zimmermann in the front seat of the car.

Ahead was the boy Mrs. Zimmermann had spotted in the crystal. It was Stan, all right, and he limped along like some kind of zombie. His short-sleeved plaid shirt hung from his shoulders in loose flapping folds, and the sneakers on his feet were torn and stained. He lurched along blindly, his arms dangling, his eyes staring, his face thin and red and sweating.

Jonathan yanked the car onto the shoulder, raising a cloud of dust, and they spilled out. He jogged ahead to Stan and put his hands on the boy's shoulders. "Stanley! Where do you think you're going?"

The exhausted Stan tried to jerk free of his hold, but he could not. Father Foley said, "Let me." With surprising strength, he lifted Stan like a rag doll and carried him back to the car. He laid the boy down and murmured a prayer before turning to Jonathan. "Give me the bottle of holy water," he ordered.

From his vest pocket, Jonathan produced a small bottle that held perhaps two ounces of holy water. The priest took it, moistened his fingers, and made the sign of the cross on Stan, touching his forehead, his chest, and each shoulder.

Stan grew rigid. His eyes flew open wide, and he screamed a high-pitched, terrifying scream. Rose Rita blanched, clapping her hands over her ears. Mrs. Zimmermann started forward, but Father Foley held up a hand to stop her. In a stern voice, he recited a ritual of exorcism, commanding the evil spirit to free Stan.

And it seemed to work. With a gasp, Stan fell silent. He closed his eyes, and when he opened them again, he struggled to sit up. "What? Who are you?" he gasped, staring at the priest. "Where am I? What's goin' on?"

"You know me, don't you?" asked Jonathan in a comforting tone.

Stan blinked. "Yeah. You're Lard—uh, I mean, you're Lewis's uncle. Wh-where am I?" His face jerked into a mask of fear. "N-not in New Zebedee? Did you bring me back to New Zebedee? I can't go there! *She's* there!"

"Who's there?" asked Mrs. Zimmermann.

Stan's eyes were wild. "The snake-lady! Her teeth—she bit me!" he wailed.

"Into the car, everyone," ordered Jonathan. "No time to waste!"

Stan stammered out an incredible story. He remembered very little of his weeks in the hospital, but he had a terrifying memory of being chased by something like a huge snake in a rainstorm. He had crouched beneath a bush to hide, and someone had called him out—a beautiful woman who promised to take him home. But—

"She bit me!" he moaned. "I felt her drinking my b-blood!"

"Where were you going?" asked Mrs. Zimmermann.

As though he were dreaming, Stan said, "Richardson's . . . Woods. I was . . . going . . . there."

"I could have figured that much," said Jonathan from behind the wheel. "Hmm. All right, here's what we will do." He drove them back to New Zebedee and parked at the curb in front of the police station. "Stan, you march right inside there and have them call your parents. And stay put until they come for you! They'll take you back to the hospital, but you'll be safe there. Understand?"

Stan was so frightened, he could barely clamber out of

the car, and then he ran to the police station on wobbling legs. Through the glass front door they saw him talking to a policeman, and then Jonathan drove off. "He should be safe enough," he said. "Now let's go to Richardson's Woods. I've got an itchy feeling that we'll find Lewis there. Father Foley, you say we're safe until tomorrow?"

"I hope so," replied the priest. "The lamia's powers are strongest at certain times and seasons of the year. She will be at her most powerful from midnight to dawn tonight. But I believe Lewis is in great danger now. She will need blood to take on enough form to fight us, and you've taken away her supply."

Rose Rita gulped hard. "You mean she might attack Lewis?"

"I believe she will," agreed the priest. His face took on an expression of anguish.

Jonathan Barnavelt floored the accelerator, and the old car sped through lengthening afternoon shadows.

They are coming.

Lewis's head spun. His vision began to clear. He still lay on the stone, with the whistle so cold on his chest that it almost burned. He raised his head with difficulty. At the foot of the stone stood the creature. She had the form of a woman, but still she was only a sheet—the sheet from his bed, Lewis dimly realized—stretched tight over a shifting figure. The eye sockets glowed red. When the thing moved, its arms and legs were wrong, as if they had no bones in them. Or as if they had the many joints of a snake.

They stopped the boy.

"S-Stan?" Lewis could speak, though his voice was a dry croak. "They s-stopped him?" He felt a little leap of hope in his heart.

No matter. You have the whistle.

Lewis shivered. The simple word sounded baleful and threatening. "I d-don't understand."

If blood cannot give me a body, the whistle can. When you blow it for the last time, my spirit can enter your body. You will not die, but you will no longer be in control of yourself. I will. They will think I am you, and I will have form and strength enough to do what must be done.

"I won't do it!" said Lewis. "You can't make me!"

You will wish to do it, returned the insinuating voice. *You will have to do it. But your earthly shell will have to perish. My spirit inside you will consume your body to ash and dust, though your spirit will live forever and will be a part of me, sharing the bodies I take, watching helplessly as I grow and grow in strength and power. But the one beneath the stone must have a body as well as a spirit, so one of the others must go there, to be imprisoned and helpless for eternity. The foolish uncle, perhaps, though I could use his magical powers . . . No, better, it will be the girl.*

It took every ounce of strength and every drop of courage in Lewis to do what he did next. He rolled sideways. The creature at his feet hissed and leaped forward, but not before Lewis was falling from the stone. He fell to the ground, and the moment he touched the earth he felt suddenly released from the thing's hold. He had landed facedown, but he sprang to his feet like a runner starting a race. Half running and half stumbling, he fled from the clearing, out into the meadow.

But the lamia reared from the tall grass ahead of him. The face formed from the sheet was wrinkled and furious, and the gaping mouth showed two curving fangs. The creature hissed at him. The grass whipped, streamers of it tearing loose and flying to the monstrous form.

Lewis backed away. The grass clung to the lamia's shape, changed it. Now it had no legs, but the trunk and tail of a monstrous serpent. It writhed forward, forcing him back. The stone touched the back of his legs, and he felt himself being forced to climb onto it. The lamia wanted him to lie down, but with all his might Lewis forced himself to stand atop the stone. He felt the monster in his mind, willing him to raise the silver whistle to his lips.

"I won't do it!" he yelled desperately. With a sudden yank, he broke the chain and flung the whistle away from him. It gleamed in the sunlight and vanished.

And he felt its weight in his pocket again.

You must.

Lewis almost sobbed. He couldn't get rid of the whistle! And the thing would force him to blow it. Then— what then? Would his mind go when the creature's spirit took over his body? Or would he be left aware but helpless?

Would he see the thing destroy his friends?

CHAPTER THIRTEEN

"I wish I'd dressed for this," grumbled Mrs. Zimmermann as she, Father Foley, Jonathan Barnavelt, and Rose Rita made their way through the meadows toward Richardson's Woods. Despite their speed, it was late afternoon by the time they came within sight of the place.

Rose Rita shuddered. The trees were dark and strange, moving and thrashing even though the wind wasn't blowing very hard. "What do we do?" she asked. "Go charging in like gangbusters? Or is there some spell or something?"

"Here," said Jonathan, handing her a small bottle. "This is holy water, and it may protect you. We all have some. Now, this creature will be tricky and sneaky, so don't let her come up on your blind side! Stick together and let's see if we can find Lewis."

Slowly, huddling together, they descended the hillside. Rose Rita looked ahead with dread. Every movement of a branch or clump of grass startled her and made her think something was about to leap out at her. She clutched the bottle hard, not sure what to do with it. Through her head ran memories of every vampire movie she had ever seen. Didn't it require a stake through the heart to kill a vampire? Or sunlight?

But the sunlight was going fast. They were in twilight by the time they got to the foot of the hill.

Jonathan shouted, "Lewis! Are you here?" in a booming voice, making Rose Rita jump a mile.

No one answered. In fact, despite the rustling of the leaves overhead, everything seemed too quiet. "Maybe he's not here," she said.

"He's here, all right," retorted Mrs. Zimmermann. "And I sense something really nasty in here with him. Come on!"

Beneath the trees it was darker still, a greenish gloom that brooded over everything. The ground underfoot turned rocky, and suddenly they emerged in the clearing.

And there was Lewis, the silver whistle raised to his lips.

Behind him was something that Rose Rita would see again and again.

In her nightmares.

Lewis stood on the stone. He was locked into place, as if his legs had become stone themselves, as if they had petrified. He held his breath. Sweat poured from his face. He clenched his teeth together, telling himself, "I won't! I won't! I won't blow this whistle!"

But as if it came up through the stone itself, the will of the lamia forced him to raise it to his lips. He felt his chest expanding. Dimly he could see his friends. Rose Rita was staring in horror at the snaky thing that coiled around the stone and reared its ghostly head behind him. Mrs. Zimmermann had raised her staff, and a brilliant purple starburst erupted from the crystal at the tip of it. Jonathan was pointing his cane and shouting magical words. And there was someone else, someone pushing past the others—Father Foley!

Blood roared in Lewis's ears. He felt cold hatred rolling from the lamia. *You! My ancient enemy!*

Desperately, Lewis pulled the tube a half inch from his lips. His breath puffed out. His arm trembled as the lamia's fierce magic forced the whistle back.

Lewis could feel the lamia's rage and its desire to destroy the old priest. He could not understand it, but it was strong, a lash of fury. And he knew that as soon as he sounded the whistle for a third time, her evil spirit would flow into his body, would make him a puppet for her to act on her hatred. He had a brief vision in his mind of his body blazing into fire, of himself leaping from the stone, destroying the magicians, swelling with their power, leaving the old man for last. He felt the silver cold on his lips and sobbed with the effort to wrench it away.

Father Foley crossed himself. "Lewis! Listen to me! You do not have to do this!"

But he did, he did.

Lewis inhaled. He would blow the whistle. He had to blow it.

In a voice of thunder, Father Foley shouted at him: "You lazy, wretched boy! How much Latin do you know? Translate! *Quantum materiae materietur marmota monax si marmota monax materiam possit meteriari?* Translate!"

Lewis's head spun. The Latin words whirled in his mind. The lamia's mind turned away from him, and toward the priest. It was as if a giant hand gripping him had loosened a little. Lewis held his breath, then under Father Foley's burning gaze he pulled the whistle away from his lips. The words. He had to translate the words. "H-hah," he stammered. "Ho-how—"

Father Foley pointed a bony finger and shouted a spell. The whistle jerked from Lewis's grasp and flew through the air. "I reclaim it!" shouted the priest. He reached out a hand to catch the silvery tube, but too late!

The lamia descended on him, a pouring horror. Lewis stared in disbelief. The sheet, the grass, all streamed against the priest, making him stagger back. The whistle tumbled.

And a hand closed on it in midair. "I've got it!" shrieked Rose Rita. She turned and ran.

As if he were a puppet whose strings had been cut, Lewis fell. He struck the stone, rolled down it again, and crashed to the ground. But now he had control of his body. He pushed himself up. Rose Rita was flying between the trees, rushing out of the grove. The priest lay crumpled, and from him flowed the form of a gigantic snake, hissing and coiling. Both Jonathan and Mrs. Zimmermann were pointing their wands at the creature and shouting magical words. Power pulsed in purple waves from Mrs. Zimmermann's staff, and white light streamed from Uncle Jonathan's cane, but neither had any effect. They dashed after the lamia as it twisted through the trees, hot on Rose Rita's heels.

The priest groaned. Lewis staggered to his side. "Father Foley—"

The old man smiled. "I have it," he said in a harsh whisper. "They cannot destroy the creature. They must destroy—" He coughed. "They must destroy the link! Tell them! Go!"

Lewis left him and ran out into the meadow. Rose Rita had reached the crown of the grassy hill, but the serpent, now an impossible thirty or forty feet long, had surrounded her with a huge coil. It rose above her, swaying. Rose Rita's eyes were wide and terrified.

Lewis ran to Mrs. Zimmermann, who was still pumping magical power against the creature. "That won't work!" he screamed. "Father Foley said to destroy the link!"

"The link?" asked Mrs. Zimmermann, not taking her eyes off the swaying monster. "What is that?"

"Lewis!" shrieked Rose Rita. "Here!" She wound up and threw.

The whistle, trailing its chain, flew toward him. The lamia struck at Rose Rita, and she fell to the earth. The forepart of the monster was no longer human. The head bore a long, blunted snout, like the head of a gigantic snake. The arms had become mere claws. But the baleful eyes still glowed red.

"The link!" shouted Lewis. He lunged forward, reaching, stretching.

The snake reared back, then struck forward.

Falling onto his stomach, Lewis caught the whistle. "This is it! This is the link!"

"Drop it!" shouted Mrs. Zimmermann. "Jonathan, gain me two seconds!"

Jonathan Barnavelt threw himself into the path of the serpent. "Oh, no you don't, Fang Face! I've got a score to settle with you. *This* is for my nephew! And *this* is specially from me!"

White fire roared from Jonathan's cane, enveloping the creature's head. It reared back, hissing, the crumpled sheet burning to black flakes. Somehow the monster kept its shape, now made up of the ashes and smoke. With a vicious swipe, it knocked Jonathan aside. Another blow of its tail sent him tumbling.

But now Mrs. Zimmermann had turned her staff to point it at the whistle. She yelled a long, complicated phrase that seemed to have words from many languages tied up into it. A thin purple stream hit the whistle.

The lamia snatched at the silver tube, but its withered little claw drew back as the whistle glowed white-hot.

Lewis winced as he heard the thing's voice in his head: *No! You cannot! I forbid you!*

As if she had heard the words too, Mrs. Zimmermann snarled, "Watch me, you scaly spirit!" And with a blast that made her arms shake, she sent a spear of brilliant purple light lancing to the ground. The whistle melted, then vaporized. A jet of silver steam shot into the air and puffed away on the breeze.

The lamia reared high over Mrs. Zimmermann, bellowing in outrage. It fell forward, and Lewis raised his arm against its deadly strike.

But it dissolved. Spears of grass showered down against his face. Flakes of burned fabric blew away on the breeze. The screams of outrage wailed away to a dying whine, like that of a mosquito.

Mrs. Zimmermann staggered, leaning on her staff. Her blue eyes were faded with exhaustion. But she extended her arm, and Lewis rushed into her embrace.

They stood there a moment, leaning on each other. Then, fearfully, they turned to discover what had happened to the others.

CHAPTER FOURTEEN

"Hey, Lewis."

Lewis froze in mid-step just outside of Heemsoth's Rexall Drug Store. Ahead of him stood Stan Peters, looking thin and haggard. "What do you want?"

Stan stared at him. "Whatcha got in the bag?"

"Some medicine and stuff," muttered Lewis. "My uncle's sick."

"Yeah." Stan took a deep breath. "Look, I know how it is to be sick. I've been pretty sick myself. So—good luck, huh?"

Lewis was on the verge of telling him to buzz off, but something in Stan's eyes pleaded with him. "Thanks," Lewis heard himself say. He walked past Stan.

"Hey, Lewis," called Stan again.

Lewis turned around. Stan had not moved. "What is it?"

Stan shrugged. "See you at the Scout meeting, okay?"

"Okay," said Lewis. He hurried on, trying to sort out his feelings. Everything was strange, as if he had been dead and had come back to life. And he couldn't tell whether he was happier or sadder to be back.

He banged through the front door of his house. Mrs. Zimmermann met him and said, "Old Grumpy Gus wouldn't stay in bed. He's stretched out on the parlor sofa."

Lewis and Mrs. Zimmermann went in to see him. Uncle Jonathan was a sight. He had lumps and bruises and scrapes, and a swollen left eye. "You two carry on as if I'm at death's door," he growled. "I'll be fine in a day or two!"

Rose Rita came in from the kitchen. She was holding a steaming mug. "Here's your chicken soup," she said. She had a couple of scrapes on her arm and one black eye. She had told her parents that she had taken a spill on her bike, something that had happened once or twice, and they had accepted that explanation. The lamia had merely swiped her aside, though, and she looked hardly the worse for wear, unlike Jonathan, who had been brutally pummeled by the angry creature.

"I brought the aspirin," said Lewis, holding out the drugstore bag.

Mrs. Zimmermann made Jonathan take a couple, and then she sighed. "What is the church going to do about replacing Father Foley?" she asked.

Jonathan shook his head. "Search me. They say he died of a heart attack, but we know better. He went when the lamia went. Until she passed from the earth, he couldn't die."

Mrs. Zimmermann shook her head. "It's like the myth of Tithonis, who asked the Greek gods for eternal life but not eternal youth. He withered and withered away, getting older, weaker, and more miserable year by year. No wonder poor Father Foley was so hard to get along with. He carried the weight of centuries on his shoulders."

"Is the lamia really gone?" asked Rose Rita. "For good?"

Mrs. Zimmermann frowned. "Well, with Father Foley's soul at rest, it can't come back to this earth, anyway. Not without that glorified magical kazoo!"

Rose Rita looked unsatisfied. "Are you really sure? I mean, you couldn't find any trace of the lamia when we first went to the grave, and then it didn't seem to trip up any of Mr. Barnavelt's magical traps."

"There's a reason for both of those things," put in Jonathan. "You see, the lamia wasn't exactly a ghost, but a spirit from the ancient times of deep magic. She had never really been alive to begin with. And Frizzy Wig was specifically trying to find ghosts at the grave."

"True," agreed Mrs. Zimmermann. "And then Furry Face set his traps to catch a magician—someone with a body, not a spirit drifting on the wind. And like all vampires, she couldn't actually come inside the house until she was invited in. She tricked Lewis into giving her the invitation. The traps would not work against a guest, you see. Just against an intruder. But to answer your real question, I'm certain that the lamia has been banished from the earth. Her tie to this world was through Father Foley and the whistle. Bless him, Father Foley gave his life to banish her. If it's any comfort, I think the old man was ready to go."

"May his soul rest in peace," said Jonathan, sipping the hot soup. "I certainly had him pegged wrong. Wish I'd had the chance to tell him that."

"Maybe he knows," said Lewis in a small voice.

"Amen to your wish," said Mrs. Zimmermann. "He certainly saved our bacon. Though I should have thought about destroying the whistle myself. Did you see what happened to the stone?"

Jonathan shook his head. "All I remember is that snaky thing whapping me. After that it's a blank until I woke up in bed with Doc Humphries taking my pulse. What happened to the stone, Haggy?"

"It got sucked down into the earth," answered Rose Rita. "As if the ground under it turned into quicksand."

"Good riddance," grumped Jonathan. "I'm only glad Lewis didn't blow that danged whistle for the third time. What was it that stopped you? Was that a magical phrase that Father Foley shouted at you? I couldn't make head or tail of it!"

Lewis gave a sad grin. "It wasn't exactly magic, but I was so scared of him that when he ordered me to translate the Latin, I had to try! I think that distracted me enough so he could levitate the whistle out of my hand."

"It wasn't real Latin, was it?" asked Rose Rita.

Mrs. Zimmermann chuckled. "It was indeed! It is a very old joke that very old Latin teachers love to give to their classes. In fact, considering Father Foley's true age, I suspect it is a positively *ancient* joke. Lewis, did you work out the translation, or shall I?"

"I think I got it," said Lewis. "'How much wood could a woodchuck chuck if a woodchuck could chuck wood?'"

Jonathan Barnavelt laughed. Then he shook his head. "Who would have thought that old priest had a sense of humor? Well, I say again, may his soul rest in peace."

And with all of his heart, Lewis agreed.